Cowboys & Vengeance

Creek

The Story of Redd Bird

The history of the black American cowboy is rarely told. When one thinks of a cowboy they think of a white man.

From the time that slavery was abolished until the late nineteenth century, there were nearly 9,000 black cowboys traveling across the western United States.

Some have heard the stories of the great Jesse Stahl. He was a Negro cowboy, who lost out on first place in a rodeo because of racism.

Stahl's name was written in history when he showed up at the next competition.

He returned to the same rodeo and entered the contest riding a horse backwards while holding a suitcase.

What about John Ware? Ware was an ex-slave from

Texas who was known as the most successful cattle rancher of his time.

Everyone has a story that has been passed down through generations and centuries, but there is one story that you have never heard of.

The story of the Redd Bird has never been told until now.

Redd's story was one of trials and triumph, losses and gains.

He met and trained some of the greatest cowboys, cowgirls and great men of the Wild West.

Redd's story has never been told, until now.

Cowboys & Vengeance

Creek

American Indian Proverb

Humankind has not woven the web of life.

We are but one thread within it.

Whatever we do to the web, we do to ourselves.

All things are bound together.

All things connect.

Chief Seattle, 1854

Chapter 1

Redd couldn't believe his luck; he had arrived at his target location a full day early.

He smiled to himself knowing that the job he had to do in the morning was going to be an easy one.

He sat on the grassy knoll staring off into the distance. The setting sun lit the Arizona horizon as if it were on fire.

He shook his head viciously, trying to push the images away from his mind.

He could hear the words of Dark Eagle, his grandfather floating in his head, "Dream your dreams with your eyes closed...but live your dreams with your eyes open".

At this moment he couldn't think about dreams, he could only think about survival.

He moved closer to the warm fire. He knew that soon he would have to put it out. The last thing he needed was to be discovered.

His line of work was a tricky one. He was grateful for his job; many of the men he knew were still doing backbreaking work in the cotton fields.

Sure it was 1889 and slavery had been abolished, but it was difficult to find work as a colored man.

Although he had the appearance of an American Indian, Redd never took any chances.

He closely resembled his grandfather with a deep red undertone that resembled fire when hit by the glare of the sun.

He was born in Alabama on a quiet Indian reservation. Tall Winged Elm lush vegetation and Sweet Gum trees surrounded the land.

He took in a deep breath trying to recall the smell of the honeysuckle flowers in his nostrils.

He could hear the rushing waters of the Choctawhatchee River.

His clan occupied the land that he tilled and plowed for hundreds of years. His grandfather shared the rich heritage of their family history.

It made him proud to know that he was living exactly like his ancestors once did.

His people believed that knowledge of the land was a form of self-preservation.

They planted large vegetable and fruit gardens in the fertile fields of their ancestors. He and Dark Eagle fished at the river daily.

Redd was his grandfather's shadow. He watched everything Dark Eagle did and mimicked it.

As the chief of the tribe the people revered him. Everyone went to him for advice.

He had a way of making people feel comfortable yet small in his presence.

The men of his tribe spent their time fishing and tending to their camp. They lived a life of simplicity that Redd longed to have again.

His mother was Muskogee Indian and his father a freed Negro slave.

His mother raised him on the reservation with the help of his uncles, aunts and clan.

He didn't know much about his father other than the fact that he was found hung outside their campsite.

Although he was a young boy he remembered seeing his mother cry for the first time in his life.

His mother rarely talked about his father, but he remembered how he looked. She had one photograph of him and she carried it everywhere.

As a young child he promised his mother that he would avenge the murder of his father.

It cut him deeply as he watched her mourn his death for her entire life.

In fact, he made it his mission to find the person who murdered him.

He promised his grandfather that he would learn to be an assassin and kill the man who killed his father.

The words of his grandfather still haunt him, "Revenge is like a slow burning fire. It consumes only one; the one who feeds the fire."

He didn't care about it consuming him. He shadowed his grandfather and watched his every move.

When he hunted, Redd was by his side. When he negotiated with the other tribes, Redd was right there.

Redd was a man because of his grandfather and his dedication to his father.

He reached in his pocket and pulled out the photo of a tall man with a bright smile and dark eyes standing next to an ox with a plow attached.

"I will find out who killed you and I will peel their skin from their bones", he said as he rubbed his hands gently across his knife.

His grandparents didn't treat him differently, in fact his relationship with Dark Eagle was the reason why he became the man he was.

He recalled his first fishing trip with his grandfather and cousin Aole.

He remembered begging his mother to go fishing when he was young.

His mother kept telling him that he had to wait until he was of age to fish.

She was a tiny woman with a soft smile and long raven hair that she wore in two braids.

Redd was her only child, named after her first love. She

was quite protective of him.

Being the daughter of the chief, she was afforded the luxury of doting upon Redd.

She tried to keep him within the confines of their home at all times.

To her dismay, he chose to follow after the men as they hunted and fished.

His grandfather promised to take him along on their first fishing trip of the year.

Since they preferred to fish in the late fall and winter, Redd came prepared.

He wore a pair of buckskin leggings and a freshly made breachcloth, thanks to his mother.

He remembered how his cousin laughed when he first saw him.

His cousin Aole was older than Redd and often teased him.

Aole was his uncle Blue Sky's son. Since they were around the same age, they were raised as brothers.

As they walked toward the river, Aole cautioned Redd about their trip.

He had been fishing with the older men since the previous winter and wanted to show off what he knew.

His grandfather reached out for the spear and began to instruct Redd on the process.

Before he could complete the lesson, Redd was in the water.

He ignored the pleas and cries for him to return to shore.

Redd returned to the shore less than an hour later, carrying his bounty of fish.

His grandfather scolded him in public for disobeying him. He made Redd sit and watch the rest of the men fish as a punishment.

Redd didn't realize it at that time, but his grandfather saw something in him. He saw the greatness of his ancestors in Redd.

He couldn't imagine his six-year-old grandson mastering the art of spear fishing.

After the day concluded, his grandfather pulled him aside and handed him the painted tail of a rabbit.

Redd stared in awe, knowing exactly what he was staring at. His grandfather was honored by his acts that day.

As he reached in his pocket and pulled out the rabbit tail, he laughed to himself.

He recalled the large spotted bass and sunfish he cleaned in front of his wide-eyed grandfather.

The look on Dark Eagle's face showed nothing but pride.

His grandfather was amazed by the things he could do at such a young age.

Sadness overtook him as he imagined what his grandfather would say about him at that moment. He had shamed his family.

He was doing things that he was never taught to do. His people were all about love and sharing. They didn't waste blood unnecessarily.

Redd shook his head as he opened his bag of arsenal.

The war clubs, sharpened ax and knife were each hidden in their compartments available for use.

He reached for the wooden tube behind his bag and pulled out an arrow.

He hummed along to the tune of an old campfire song as he prepared for the next day.

Rubbing the slimy substance along the sides of the arrow, he paid attention not to let any touch his skin.

The poisonous secretions he used from the Black Bottom Spider could kill an elephant.

He chuckled to himself as he thought; he only needed it to kill a 250-pound man.

Chapter 2

He steadied himself as he climbed higher in the Sycamore tree.

He could nearly see the entire forest from his vantage point, but he only needed to see two feet in front of him.

His target was busy cleaning up his camp. He didn't notice Redd watching him closely.

Redd had been hot on his trail for nearly a month. He received almost $20 for the head of Bo Law, a local town sheriff.

Bo owed money to the wrong man and Redd was going to settle Bo's debt and get paid at the same time.

He shuddered thinking about the man who hired him for the job. He was a short white man with bright red hair and a large stomach.

He was a banker from Oklahoma, with deep pockets.

He liked to be referred to as The Boss, but Redd didn't address no one as boss.

He called him by his last name, Howard.

He wouldn't consider calling him anything different.

Howard threw his weight around town, had people terrified of him.

He had the finest woman in town too. She was an American Indian woman with a small stature. Wilma reminded Redd of his mother.

Every time he saw her, he felt the strong desire to rescue her. He wanted to whisk her away from Howard's chubby little hands.

He knew that he had nothing to offer her. He found himself staring at her far too long when he visited Howard.

Howard knew that he had a beauty on his hands, although he treated her terribly.

He yelled at her and on several occasions he witnessed him hit her.

It took everything in Redd to not protect Wilma. But she was not his. She belonged to another. Someone that was more powerful than Redd.

He had more money and more pull, but no strength.

Redd could look into his eyes and tell that he was a wimp of a man. He used his money and guards to scare people, but no one scared Redd.

He did respect Howard, however. A disrespectful Negro was a dead man in these parts. Even Redd knew about self-preservation.

Although he was a squirrel of a man, Redd enjoyed working for him. He paid on time and in full.

There were many times when the payments from Howard kept him fed on a cold winter's night.

It was hard to find work out in the West in the winter.

His grandfather had been dead for over a year and had begged him to live the life of his dreams.

When Dark Eagle was ill, he honored Redd's uncle Wise Bear with the position as chief.

Although, the others were not happy with the selection, they respected Wise Bear.

It wasn't until their land began to shrink that they noticed who the culprit was. Wise Bear had sold the majority of their land for riches.

When Redd confronted his cousin, things began to deteriorate rapidly.

Redd wanted to secure the legacy that his grandfather passed on to him, but Wise Bear had different plans.

When he awoke one morning to the screams of his mother, Redd didn't know what to do.

He came face to face with Wise Bear, himself. He was ready to square off with him.

Wise Bear had different plans, "leave this place and I won't slice her throat" he said as he held Redd's mother by her hair.

Redd lunged toward him, only to be kicked in the chest by Wise Bear's henchmen. "Leave Redd!" his mother yelled as Redd continued to fight back.

He woke up the following morning on the outside of the camp. His cousin Aole was standing over him.

"You shouldn't have challenge him," he said shaking his head in despair. "I'll take care of your mother. If you stay here you will be killed" he said assuredly.

Redd trusted his cousin, but the thought of leaving his mother didn't sit well with him.

He kissed his mother good-bye, knowing that he would never see her again.

She held his hand tightly and stared in his eyes. "For you" she said as she handed him an object wrapped in silk.

When he unwrapped the silk his hands trembled. He was holding his father's knife. He recognized it immediately.

He hugged his mother as she whispered in his ear, "Remember the teachings of your youth", she said as she kissed his cheek.

He knew exactly what she meant. He had to take care of himself, now. He had to be a man and make his own way.

He had no idea what his way really was.

It wasn't until his grandfather visited him in his sleep that evening that he realized his destiny. He had to leave his homeland and set out on his own.

He wondered if his grandfather was ashamed of whom he had become.

A hired assassin, he was a man that was not seen nor heard. He moved under the cover of the darkness and slept under the stars.

He didn't enjoy being an assassin, but it was a means to an end.

He could see the disapproval on his grandfather's face as he released the bow.

Taught by some of the best hunters around, Redd was a skilled as a surgeon with the bow and arrow.

He didn't stay to watch the body drop.

Redd was hired for his precision.

He knew that Bo was dead.

Redd remained at the top of the tree holding on to the thickest branch.

He scanned the area surrounding Bo's camp, searching for stragglers.

If it was one thing he learned in his line of work, you never know who's watching you.

Never Look Back

"Looking behind I am filled with gratitude. Looking forward I am filled with vision. Looking upwards I am filled with strength. Looking within, I discover peace."

Creek Indian Proverb

Chapter 3

Redd was on a mission. As he raced back to camp and prepared for his next assignment, Redd surveyed the land.

It would have been nice to live there. It was something about the way the sunset behind the hills that reminded him of home.

His horse, Midnight was watching him as he drank slowly from the water bucket.

She was a sturdy horse with a deep shiny black mane the shade of coal. He won Midnight in a game of cards at a Saloon in Idaho.

He named her Midnight because of her color. It didn't hurt that he won her at the stroke of midnight.

He knew then that she would be a lucky horse.

Redd had been all over the plains and western states searching for his family. He didn't want to admit it, but he had given up hope of finding them.

He chastised himself for leaving his mother. He knew that she needed care and his cousin's wife was a nurse. He knew that he did what was best for her.

Redd chuckled as he rubbed Midnight's back. "Alright, ole girl. It's time to saddle up," he said as he continued packing.

Redd threw his knapsack on the back of the horse saddle and took one last look around. He had to return to Montana to collect his payment and set out on a new job.

He reached in his pocket and pulled out a small piece of paper. The paper had four names written on it.

As he crossed the second name off the list he breathed a deep sigh.

Howard promised him additional money if he reached all of the targets on the list before winter. Redd was trying to do better than that.

As he and Midnight rode along the dusty road, he let out a sigh of relief. He didn't have many names left on his list.

After he hit his last target he planned to collect his riches and settle down.

The thought of being a wealthy rancher with all the cattle, horses and asses he could count made him misty eyed.

He thought about his grandfather and the reservation.

After 20 years of searching he would finally be home.

He wiped a tear and let out a yell, "Yah" he said as he gently nudged Midnight on her left side, urging her to speed up.

He had to get to Montana before his target left.

I Am Not There

Don't stand by my grave and
weep, for I am not there.

I do not sleep.

I am thousand winds that blow.

I'm the diamond's glint on snow.

I am the sunlight on ripened grain.

I am the gentle autumn's rain.

Don't stand by my grave and cry.
I am not there. I did not die.

Indian Proverb

Chapter 4

Chip looked around frantically. He didn't know what was going on.

He left his buddy at the campsite and went to get more firewood only to find him dead with an arrow in his heart.

He had been searching for clues for over four hours. Being Sheriff of the small town he couldn't help but begin an investigation.

The arrow that pierced his friend's heart was the only clue that he could locate. Staring down at the body, he wiped a single tear away.

Bo wasn't the greatest guy on earth, but he was his brother. He couldn't believe someone had killed his baby brother.

Chip knew that pitching camp out in the middle of nowhere was a bad idea, but his brother seemed eager to rest.

He promised his mother on her deathbed that he would take care of his youngest brother.

As she lie on the cot, sick and yellow with jaundice he made that promise to her.

As his brother lay on his back with his eyes fixated on the sky, Chip said a prayer.

He apologized to his mother for not keeping his promise and then while no one was watching, he cried.

He felt terrible as he fastened his brother's shirt and closed his eyes.

He didn't want to remove the arrow, but he had to. If he wanted to find the bastard who killed his brother, he had to work the case.

Chip had been a man of the law for nearly a decade. His father was a Sheriff as well, killed in the line of duty.

For as long as he could remember, Chip wanted to be just like his father.

Chip stared at the arrow and imagined how his brother was sitting. He sat down in the same position, right next to his brother.

As he sat there, he began calculating the possible distance and direction of the arrow.

He looked up at the tree and gasped.

There was no way someone could have sat in those trees. They were large elm trees with wide, then branches.

Someone had to be stealth like a cat to climb the tree and sit there long enough to shoot an arrow. After taking in the entire scene he closed his eyes.

He envisioned someone sitting high in the elm tree looking down upon his brother.

He pulled out his compass and walked towards the left of their campsite.

As he continued walking in the direction of the compass he counted his steps. He stopped when he reached step 120.

The area was littered with small leaves. "This is the spot", he declared aloud.

He would bet anything that the person who killed his brother hid directly above where he was standing.

He looked above where he stood. He looked around the

area, searching desperately for a clue.

As he turned to leave the area he nearly jumped out of his skin.

There it was, sitting at the base of a tree. It was nearly hidden by fallen leaves.

A small white feather from the great bald eagle.

He picked it up and smelled it. He tucked the arrow in his pocket and continued searching the area.

Something told him that he wasn't up against an ordinary killer.

He returned to the campsite an hour later. When he pulled out the arrow he stared at the feathers on the tip.

They were an exact match to the feather he found on the

trail.

Chapter 5

The dust caught in his throat as he struggled to hold on to the wild horse.

The large creature thrashed and reared, trying desperately to free himself of Redd.

Redd didn't care. Breaking in wild horses was no harder than breaking in a young woman. All it took was patience.

He hummed an old tune as the horse continued bucking and blowing out exasperated air.

"Whoa" he kept repeating as he pulled gently on the reins and squeezed the sides of the horse with his boots.

To his relief the horse finally settled down. Redd ushered the beautiful Mustang into the stable.

He had been working with the horse for days trying to break him. Finally, he was getting somewhere.

Redd loved the money, but despised the backbreaking work of being a cowboy. Since arriving in town months before, he had taken on many odd jobs.

He found that he received more respect in the West as a cowboy than he did in the south.

The skills that Dark Eagle taught him came in handy on the frontier. It earned him more respect from the white ranch owners.

They scoffed at the work that they slid to the Negros and Indians.

Redd worked for an old rancher who was kind enough to allow him to build camp on his property while he worked.

Redd had been working for the old man for nearly a year. His plan was to earn enough money to return to Alabama.

Returning to Alabama had always been his goal. He wanted to save his mother from Wise Bear's grasp and take back the reservation.

That was the reason why he found himself high tailing it towards his next target.

Once he completed the list, his job was done in the West.

He would have enough money to do exactly what he needed to do. The only thing holding him back was his penchant for revenge.

Although, there were only two names left on his list, he really had four people to take down.

Before he could sleep soundly those four people would have to meet their demise.

He thought about his goals as he and Midnight rode through the prairie heading towards the dessert.

Chapter 6

Chip wiped away the sweat as he continued digging the hole for his brother.

He couldn't leave his brother lying out for the buzzards.

Although, he had revenge on his mind he was mourning too deeply that day to think straight.

His brother was the last surviving member of his family.

It killed him to drop his brother's body in the ground.

As he said a prayer, he reached in his knapsack and pulled out the feather. He would continue his hunt the following day.

The next day he was on the trail before the sun rose completely.

Chip had called on his entire force, which include his dog and horse.

Dusty and Drake were his best friends. He attributed a great deal of his solved cases to their efforts.

True his town rarely saw murders. Bo's murder was the first case he had in years, but he was determined to solve it.

He wasn't going to solve it for himself, but for his poor mother. She raised nine children on her own and buried all but two.

Bo and Chip were the only two children who lived to adulthood. Bo was her baby. She doted upon him and made sure that Chip took care of his brother.

His brother Bo was an outlaw. A man who committed more crimes than Chip had solved, but he was a good man.

"Alright now" he called out to Dusty as he watched Drake kick and snort in the distance.

He had given the feather to Dusty for a good sniff. Dusty made a big deal out of sniffing the feather and looking around. He then returned to the ground, sniffing for a scent.

"What ya got?" he asked as he watched Dusty's tail shoot straight in the air. He knew that he was on to something.

With Dusty in the lead, Chip ran as fast as he could.

He tried to keep up with the dog but found himself losing strength as they continued running.

When they finally stopped Dusty walked to an area in the middle of a clearing of trees. He saw the remains of a campfire.

"This was his camp," he said as he looked around, searching for clues. He found another feather in the search.

As he stood in the middle of the campsite contemplating, he heard Dusty in the distance barking.

He ran towards Dusty and found him holding an arrow with a feather on it, and a picture of an eagle on the sharpened flint.

Chapter 7

He could hear them creeping behind him as he stood in the forest. He was holding onto his knife, clenching it so tightly blood trickled down his fingers.

He stood silent, listening for the sound of rustling behind the trees. As soon as he saw the whites of his eyes he let the arrow go.

"Swif" the arrow made a loud noise as it sailed through the air and hit its desired target. He heard the man fall to the ground with a loud thud.

As he ran towards the figure on the ground, he tried his hardest to remain silent. "Quiet storm" his grandfather used to whisper as they hunted.

To him it meant that the most deadly attacks were stealth and silent.

As he turned the warm heavy body over, he struggled to remove the mask.

The masked stSheriff who was stalking him had finally been taken down.

As he removed the mask, he gasped and stumbled backwards. Staring back at him were the eyes of his father.

He screamed and opened his eyes. It was all a dream. He wiped the sweat away from his brow. He had been fighting in his sleep, again.

He let out a loud sigh, that same damn dream, He didn't know what it meant.

The worse thing of all was he felt powerless. Redd rarely slept because his nightmares kept him wide-awake.

His grandfather told him to chase his dreams; he didn't

give him any advice about his nightmares.

He couldn't stop it from happening and he couldn't interpret it.

Blazing Sun, his great aunt had the power of dream interpretation.

Every morning someone was waiting outside her home, searching for an answer to his or her dreams.

Blazing Sun was the only resource his people used for predictions and interpretation. She was a seer.

She had the ability to look in the eyes of a person and see their future, years ahead. She charted the stars and created her own version of Astrology.

He longed to be back with his family again. He missed those times. Redd chuckled at the thought.

He tried to settle his mind and fall back into a deep sleep but it was impossible.

As he plotted and planned the next day in his head, he drifted off to sleep.

An hour later, the sounds of Midnight snoring woke him from his restless sleep.

Aggravated he stood and began to pray to his ancestors. He wanted an answer from his grandfather.

He needed to know the next direction to go.

His grandfather led him around the dry countryside. He trusted the spirit of his grandfather to lead him.

Dark Eagle was helping him on his mission to find his father's killer.

His prayer to the ancestors was to avenge his father's death and he knew that his grandfather was his spirit guide.

Chapter 8

Chip rubbed the arrow between his fingers as walked through the swinging doors of the Saloon.

"Howdy!" he hollered out as he walked around the bar and took a seat. "Howdy!" they all yelled in unison.

He loved Minnie's Spot. It was the only Saloon in the area that welcomed Negros with open arms.

Minnie's Spot was owned by a short, gray haired Negro woman in her 50s, named Minne. Minnie was a sweet lady with a touch of spice.

She had a mouth like a man and the face of one as well. Minnie wasn't pretty, but she was pretty resourceful.

Minnie sold moonshine and girls at her Spot and she made great money doing it.

When he entered the smoky room he noticed that it was occupied with the usual suspects. His eyes searched the room for Minnie.

He saw her standing in the middle of the floor wearing a short red dress and slippers. She was a sight for sore eyes.

Her face was made up with powder and she wore a wig that nearly covered her entire face. Minnie was good to Chip, though.

She always had a kind word and a warm plate available for Chip. He appreciated it. In return he showed his appreciation for Minnie in the bedroom.

He tried not to think about it, let alone speak on it. Minnie sashayed over towards him and placed her thick, pudgy hands on his shoulder.

"You came to visit me?" she asked in a husky voice. He shook his head in refusal.

"Not this time, Minnie" he said sadly as she walked away, signaling a waitress to help him.

Chip tipped his hat at the sultry waitress and ordered his favorite drink, "Whiskey?" she asked before he could open his mouth.

He nodded and lit the long tobacco cigarette. His mind had been preoccupied with dangerous thoughts for days. He felt empty without his brother, Bo.

"Howdy Chip" he heard as he felt a slap on his back. He turned to face one of his best friends, Bud.

Bud noticed the look of concern on Chip's face. "You alright?" he asked as he ordered a shot of Whiskey for himself and a refill for Chip.

"Bo was murdered yesterday" he said sadly as Bud shot

him a wide-eyed stare.

"Outlaw?" he asked as Bud nodded. That was his brother Bo's nickname. He shook his head in disgust.

"Do you know who did it?" he asked concerned. "No, but I found this", Chip answered showing him the feather.

He told his friend about the way he found his brother, dead with an arrow in his heart. Chip continued talking as he watched Bud rub his beard in confusion.

"Red skin?" he said under his breath. "I believe so" Chip responded. "Look at this" he said handing him the arrow for closer inspection.

He took in a deep inhale and held the feather up to the light and shook his head.

The guy sitting next to him on the barstool stared at the feather and made a remark. "I've seen that before" he said shaking his head.

"Bald eagle" he said as he continued gulping his drink. "Mark of the assassin" he said as he gripped the arrow in his dirty hands.

"An assassin" Chip questioned with a strained look on his face. Someone hated his brother enough to hire an assassin.

At that moment he planned to not only kill the assassin but his boss. They would all die by his hands, he vowed.

Being the son of slaves, Chip was raised to know two things were important; his work and his word.

Chip watched as Bud inspected the feather with curiosity.

Chip was confident that Bud would be able to help him find out something about the arrow or Bo's killer.

Bud was the type of person who never stayed in one place too long. Bud, Chip and Bo were friends from many years back.

They hung together as kids.

He stood in the middle of the Saloon and held the arrow and feather high in the air. "Alright listen up.

Those red bastards put a whole in Bo's heart.

We need to find the red skin that killed him and hang him high" he yelled as the others raised their mugs of beer in agreement.

They huddled together at the front of the bar to take a look at the commotion.

One fella standing near the front of the bar called out, "Anyone heard of Redd Bird?" he asked as they all mumbled under their breath.

A hush fell over the Saloon as they listened to Stinky
Pete tell the story. "I worked with him on a ranch a few
winters back. I watched Redd Bird kill two men with his
bare hands" he said showing the men by wringing his
hands together.

"Man was on his back and Redd stood up to him," he
said in a matter of fact way. "He was so quick with it. We
were herding cattle and Old man Lowre came rushing up
the hill with out pay. He said he couldn't pay us all of our
money, cause he caught one of us slacking on the job,"
he said.

"They always do that" someone called out from the
crowd as the rest of the crowd agreed in unison.

"Redd climbed down from the horse and walked right up
to Lowre. He asked about his money again and Lowre
spit in his face" he said as the men all groaned together.

"I watched him grab Lowre by his throat and snap his neck before I could hop off my horse" he said in a fearful tone. "His boy came running down the hill and tried to attack Redd. Redd took him down too" he said loudly.

"I bet this feather belongs to him" he said assuredly.

The men looked around at each other. All filled with liquor and adrenaline, they pushed aside the man's gentle warning.

"Is anyone in here afraid?" he demanded as the men yelled, "NO!" in response to his question.

"Then we shall find this Redd Bird and peel his skin from his body!" Bud yelled.

"We shall leave tomorrow before sunrise!" he yelled. "Everyone get your guns ready!" he yelled as he held his Winchester rifle high in the air.

Chapter 9

Redd pulled the reins gently as Midnight slowed to a complete stop. They were riding for hours and now it was time to setup camp.

He never rode after sunset. It was an unwritten rule for black men. He preferred to pitch a tent and set himself up for the night, instead.

There was no law around those parts and he knew that even if there were, they'd be no benefit to him.

Besides Midnight needed to rest. He trotted for hours through the plains. Redd was pleased to be making good time.

To him, time was of the essence. There was no challenge he wouldn't accept.

As he prepped the fire for dinner, he recalled his

experiences on the road.

When he first set out on his own, Redd was eager to make money.

He traveled throughout the plains avoiding most of the southern states searching for work.

After the Civil War relations were still uneasy in the South. It was hard to find work and no one was eager to hire a Negro anyway.

Many of the freed slaves and other Negros chose to go west for work.

There was a great cattle boom during the time and many found good work and great pay.

It was sheer luck that got him into being a Cowboy. While drinking one evening at a small watering hole, he overheard a conversation that changed his life.

Two men were talking about the job openings at a local farm. The rancher was searching for a dozen cowboys and was willing to pay top dollar for the experienced ones.

Redd continued drinking and listening as the men continued talking. He memorized the address and the following morning showed up at the ranch.

The rancher had the men herd over a thousand cattle that evening. Redd did his job so smoothly the rancher came to him at the end of the day.

Redd worked for the rancher off and on for nearly three winters. Being a cowboy he could travel from place to place and always find work, but there was nothing like a steady pay.

He made great money at the job and he felt like he was doing something honorable or at least legal.

Redd was a cowboy by nature. Growing up he learned how to break horses and corral herds.

The backbreaking work wasn't terrible, he was used to working hard.

He got a thrill out of breaking in horses and became great at it.

The money was great and he was able to pay for enough whiskey and women to keep himself satisfied.

Most of the places where he found work had at least two Saloons or at least a watering hole where he could grab a drink.

The special places offered women and drinks. Those were the ones that he liked to visit.

He enjoyed spending time with women, but the last thing he needed was a wife.

He wasn't ready for one. He patted his side pocket where the list rested safely and smiled to himself.

Soon he would be presenting his boss with the completed list and he would receive the rest of his money.

Redd was so good, Howard advanced him $60 for the job.

He was disappointed that had already spent a great deal of his advance.

Whiskey and women were also the reason why half of his advance was missing.

He didn't mind.

Chapter 10

By the time Chip left the Saloon he was feeling much better. In fact, he was feeling so good, some of his buddies had to help him to his horse.

Part of the reason was the whiskey. The other reason was his partners. He was so glad to have the bunch of outlaws around him.

They were always looking for something to get into and Chip needed their help.

Out in those parts there was only one code that they all lived by, even men of the law.

An eye for an eye was the code they lived by. The men drank in the Saloon for hours and planned their attack on Redd.

Chip climbed on Drake's back and tried to steady himself.

The men laughed loudly as he slumped too far to the right and fell to the ground.

He groaned as Drake kicked dust in his face. Bud threw him across his horse and climbed on the back without a thought.

He felt terrible for his friend. He bought him drinks the entire night out of pity.

He looked around staring at the group of scums he was surrounded by. Redd better watch his back, he thought as he stared at his buddies.

A group of five men dressed in jeans with pockets dragging from the weight of their guns.

He knew his buddies were all armed with their trusty Colt .45 revolvers and knives.

Every one of them had seen the inside of plenty of jails.

Each one was responsible for the death of hundreds of men.

There was quick draw Walt, who could pull out a gun in less than three seconds.

He once shot three men and two horses before his opponents could pull their guns.

He also knew that big John Boy wouldn't shy away from a good fight.

As Negros they knew the importance of sticking together and being prepared at all times.

The men earned respect throughout the Western states because of their strength and talents.

They agreed to help him find the son of a bitch who killed his brother.

He was ready to capture him, skin him and hang him high.

They already knew enough about him to know where to find him and they would be hot on his tail, before he knew it.

Strength

Be strong

When you are weak

Be brave

When you are scared

Be humble

When you are victorious

Creek Indian Proverb

Chapter 11

The small wooden building sat in the middle of town.

He could tell by the amount of horses tied to the posts in front of Ray Bean's Saloon that the place was pretty crowded.

He shrugged and took a deep inhale of the long cigarette hanging from his mouth. He rarely smoked.

Redd enjoyed a good smoke before and after a contract was completed.

Murder was such an adrenaline rush to him, he couldn't help himself.

The large hand written signs advertised Ice and beer in large letters.

He began to walk up the rickety wooden steps of the building, eyeing the dusty loiterers standing nearby.

He tipped his hat at the three fellas sitting at the small wooden table on the porch of Bean's.

Bean's was a great place to visit for all of the luxuries that life had to offer. Every man had his addiction satisfied at Bean's.

He had plenty of beautiful girls, enough beer to drown a bear and the best tables in town. Bean's specialized in three-card mote, Faro and small poker tables.

It was the best place to be in town, if you didn't have a penchant for gambling big and losing bigger.

Little knew that old man Howard owned an interest in

Bean's Saloon.

Redd made a great living when Bean's customers bit off more than they could chew.

Bean's was the place where men like Earl lost their life possessions and their families.

Redd shrugged off the concern as continued walking around the porch, searching for buddies of Earl.

He stood at the front door of the Saloon and took a deep breath. His target sat inside the Saloon at the barstool.

Based on how he barely balanced himself on the barstool, Redd knew that he had him.

He calculated that it wouldn't be long before he would stumble out of the dusty place.

Redd would be ready for him. He surveyed his surroundings. It was long after sunset and he was chastising himself for being out, but he had a job to do.

The stars sparkled with the same mischief in Redd's eyes as he contemplated Earl's death.

He could hear the loud music coming from the piano and imagined the can-can girls sashaying about.

He wished that he could go inside and enjoy himself.

As he walked away from the window he promised himself that he would return.

He needed to let some smoke off.

Heading towards the corral of horses, he found the horse that his target rode in on.

The third name on his list was once a successful man.

Redd felt bad about carrying out the contract. He didn't have a problem with the poor sap that he had to kill.

He just owed the wrong man too much money.

His boss wanted him killed execution style. Redd didn't mind that part. He just hated getting close to his targets.

An execution with his Colt.45 meant that he had to get close enough to get blood on him.

He hated blood, the sight, smell or thought of it made him sick to his stomach.

He started to reach for his bow and remembered that his boss instructed him to do everything by the book.

As he rubbed the mane of the Chocolate Mustang tied in the corral he hummed a song.

He hummed the same song every time he finished a contract. It was soothing to him.

Not that he needed anything to keep him calm.

This was Redd's specialty.

As Earl stumbled out of the swinging wooden doors, Redd was waiting for him. He cleared his throat making sure he got Earl's full attention.

When Earl heard the noise he jumped back and nearly fell to the ground.

The cowboys leaving with Earl noticed Redd and immediately raised their hands in surrender. Redd nodded at them, motioning for them to scat.

He almost chuckled watching them hustle out of Redd's way. One of them stumbled and fell in a dusty heap near his horse.

Redd noticed all of this from the corner of his eye. He never took his eyes off of Earl.

His left hand rested on his pistol. He flicked his pinky finger in anticipation, waiting on Earl to make a move.

The two men faced each other as others around the Saloon began to scatter. Everyone knew about Redd.

Folks knew when they saw Redd, someone was about to die. They generally stayed out of the way, making sure they weren't on Redd's list.

He could hear the cowboys running inside and warning others about his presence.

That didn't matter to him. The only that that concerned Redd was his countdown.

In his head he counted to ten. When he reached ten, he winked at Earl.

Before Earl's buddies could climb on their horses and scatter, Earl was dead.

Earl fell to the ground in loud dusty, thud.

The last thing witnesses saw was Redd and Midnight trotting off into the night, leaving behind only a one thing.

Redd's signature feather.

Indian Theory of Existence

Everything on Earth has a purpose,

Every disease an herb to cure it, and every person a mission.

Chapter 12

The bright sunshine stung his eyes like a thousand bees. His head was pounding and his mouth was as dry as the dessert.

Chip chastised himself for drinking the way he had done the previous night.

He needed the release, though.

He was grateful for his buddies. They were going to help him find that red skin joker and Chip would finally have his revenge.

He walked towards the water basin where Drake was drinking and splashed cold water on his face.

He needed to be alert. The fellas would be arriving soon.

They planned their attack and would be ready for Redd when he returned to Montana.

As he prepared for the journey, memories of his brother his him like a ton of bricks.

He remembered his brother and family on the farm. They spent so much time in the stables with the horses, they could sense how the horses felt.

His brother Bo had such a gift with the animals.

He was able to break a new horse in record time, because he sensed their feelings.

He was an exceptional man, though he was an outlaw that stayed in trouble.

Chip rescued his brother from danger so often he just knew that he would be there to protect him forever.

Bo had problems with gambling. It was a disease, passed down from his father and grandfather.

He remembered witnessing the men coming for his father.

His father owed a debt so large that it cost him his life. Bo watched as his mother worked her fingers to the bone as a seamstress and a maid.

She tried her hardest to feed her children and provide for them.

He wondered if his father had been alive, if Bo would have turned out the way he did.

He knew that Bo had a strong relationship with their father. It crushed him to have to bury him.

When Bo ran off at the age of 11 it was Chip who stayed around and took care of their mother.

The other children slowly began to disappear, die off from war or disease, leaving only Chip and Bo.

Some of his siblings moved away and promised to never return.

The West was a great place to find work, an even better place to get into some trouble, but it was a horrible place to raise a family.

His siblings blamed their hard life on the west. Chip always considered that shameful.

He blamed his hard life on his father's addictions.

As he sat in front of the fire, sharpening his knives and preparing his ammunition he silently cried.

He wanted to avenge his brother's death, but he didn't know if he had it in him.

Sure, he was a man that had killed before, but he wasn't sure about this Redd fella.

He talked about killing him and skinning him like an animal, but the more he heard about Redd the more afraid he became.

The men at the bar talked about Redd as if he were something to be in awe of.

As the men swapped and shared their stories, Chip grew nervous.

Any man capable of killing ten men with one revolver and a bow and arrow, by himself was a force to be reckoned with.

Listen

Listen

Or

Thy Tongue

Will keep thee

Deaf

Indian Proverb

Chapter 13

"Grab 'em, Redd" he heard as the trail boss watched them hustle after the horses.

He ran towards the bucking Bronco and pitched the rope, aiming for his neck.

The moment the rope caught on the horse, he pulled back.

The horse slowed down in time for Redd to hop on his back.

"Yah!" he yelled slapping the sides of the horse with his boots. Redd took off riding the horse at high speed, feeling free as a bird.

The horse had been ridden plenty of times, he just didn't trust the trail boss. Some of the horses just seemed to act up just for the hell of it.

He shook his head in disgust as he tied the horse to the post in the stable.

This was the third horse he had to break in that week. He was exhausted, but looking forward to the pay.

As he and the other cowboys stood in line for their pay they all chatted about their day.

Some of the men talked about what they planned to do with their pay.

One cowboy named Ernest called out, "I'm taking my loot and heading out to Missouri.

It should be nice and cold there by now," he said as the other men nodded in agreement.

They chased the seasons, searching for ranchers or owners who needed their services.

That was the life of a cowboy. Never in one place for too long.

All they needed was their horse and a bottle of whiskey to keep them warm at night.

Cowboys didn't ask for much. Redd was starting to tire of the Cowboy lifestyle.

He was searching for something different.

One of the tall Cowboys standing nearby called out to him, "Something bothering you Redd?" he asked with a concerned look on his face.

Redd nodded and tried to walk off. He didn't know those guys well.

Although they kept each other company and generally looked out for each other, he preferred to stay to himself.

He enjoyed the stories that they told by the campfire late at night. Those were the only times that they had an opportunity to talk.

The trail boss worked them so hard, they didn't have any time for anything besides work. The men banned together and stopped for lunch at the same time.

This way the entire job would shut down and no one man would have to face the trail boss's wrath.

Although none of the men were afraid of him, they knew to keep their tongues around the white man.

For Redd it was a difficult task. His grandfather reminded him to remain patient and humble. A strong man is judge by his humility not his might.

But Redd was also a headstrong fire red Indian, he wasn't going to let anyone disrespect him.

He didn't know how to tell the men that he was in search of something different.

As they sat around the campfire that evening, Redd tried to seem interested in their conversations.

He didn't want anyone questioning his mood.

Cowboys felt uneasy around quiet moody people.

They were never sure if they could trust someone who held their tongue all the time.

Redd knew that there was a fine line between being safe and being himself.

By nature, Redd wasn't a talkative man. He didn't seek

attention and preferred to stay alone.

His big break came the following day. The trail boss and the owner of the ranch were talking in front of the stalls.

Really, they were watching the boys work. Redd continued about his work, not paying them any attention, when he heard his name.

"Get to work, Redd!" he turned and looked at his beet faced boss and continued walking the horse that he had recently broken.

The trail boss, decided to react by running down the hill and throwing his boot at Redd.

"I told ya, Nigger. Get to work" he yelled as Redd reacted immediately.

He grabbed the man by his throat and watched as he took his last breath, right there in his hands.

Redd let the body drop and walked off the ranch as the other workers stared in awe.

He could hear them yelling for him to run away.

Redd didn't care about running away. He didn't allow anyone to disrespect him.

"Hey!" he heard from the top of the hill. Redd shrugged his shoulders, thinking about the fact that he would just have to kill two people in one day.

As he walked towards his horse, the boss approached him.

Redd was ready for him. His Colt .45 was tucked between his rope belt and pants.

His hands instinctively touched the gun as the man walked closer to him.

"I got a job for you" he said pointing at Redd. Redd stared at the man, wondering what type of job he had in store for him.

He could only imagine what the boss had in mind.

The boss offered his hand to Redd as Redd stared down at it. He finally took a deep breath and shook the chubby hands of the red faced man.

"I'm Boss man Howard. I like how you handle yourself. " he said nodding towards the body of the slain trail boss.

"You aint got no fear in ya. Do ya boy?" he asked as he chomped down on his cigar. Redd nodded without responding.

"I could use a man with no fear. How much do you make here, son?" he asked as Redd continued walking.

He tried to keep pace with Redd as he talked. "I am a business man, and sometimes I need my business handled without getting my hands dirty" he said smiling at Redd.

Redd continued to nod, listening to the man speak. He was once told that a wise man found more value in listening than speaking.

It was always good to listen to someone speak as opposed to doing the talking all the time.

You get a better understanding of where they are coming from.

By the end of the day, Redd was $100 richer. The cowboys and cowhands had been sworn to secrecy as they buried their trail boss.

Old man Howard kept his word. He said nothing about what he witnessed.

That was the day that Redd's life changed forever. Redd was grateful for that moment.

He turned in his cowboy rope for his bag of tricks, as he liked to refer to it.

Follow the Heart

" Certain things catch your eye,
but pursue only those that
capture the heart"

American Indian Proverb

Chapter 14

Chip rode along with the guys in silence. His heart was so heavy it could've burst.

All the fellas from the GSheriff Gang joined him in his fight for his brother.

They were six strong and they couldn't wait to get to Redd Bird.

They had their man Ant who was the tracker of the group. He could track a person better than Dusty, Chip's old hound.

Chip heard stories about how Ant was robbed at a Saloon playing poker one night.

By the time he realized that the game was fixed, the winner had ducked out the back with his earnings.

As the legend goes, the winner woke up in the middle of the night and stared down the barrel of Ant's gun.

Ant tracked the man over 200 miles in one night, with no dog or help. He shot the man in the bed with his wife, gathered his earning and left.

Each one of the men he was with had a legendary story such as Ant's. They all had a story that would make an ordinary man shudder.

Their stories filled Chip with a sense of pride.

He knew that there was no room for failure in this mission. With this group of goons, he was assured that they would make it through unscathed.

He was in the company of some of the greatest trackers,

trappers, killers and gun slingers in the west.

This was a trip that he planned to be a quick one. They had it all mapped out.

The trip would take nearly two days, but they were ensured that they would make it there on time.

One of the fellas worked the Hiplachee trail with a field hand from one of Howard's farms.

He knew where Howard lived.

The plan was to post up near the Howard ranch and wait for Redd to return.

They didn't know how much time they had, or if Redd had already been there, but they knew one thing for sure.

They were all willing to die trying.

They were riding from upper Nevada to Montana in search of Redd.

They were on a mission to find Redd Bird and they would be successful.

He hummed songs from his childhood, hoping to bring the spirit of his brother closer to him.

He imagined his brother riding by his side.

They were riding under the cloak of darkness, allowing the moon to light their paths.

He took in the scenery all around him. The rocky terrain was beautiful behind the midnight blue sky.

He couldn't help but admire the beauty of nature.

Finally, he felt the presence of his brother, ushering him on.

They were just outside the Bitter Root Mountains of Idaho, when they decided to rest and make camp.

The air was crisp for the middle of November, so they built a fire large enough to keep them all warm.

Working together, swiftly they pitched a tent and set up the area for the night.

Arlen GSheriff, the oldest in the GSheriff gang, decided to prepare a meal for the group of men.

As they chowed down on cowboy beans and wagon train biscuits, they took turns telling stories about Bo.

They laughed as they talked about Bo entering the rodeo for the first time. Bo had been drinking, as usual.

Full of whiskey and pride he entered the rodeo while challenging a Mexican rider.

He thought he had the upper hand, until it was his turn to ride.

They howled as they talked about how the bull threw Bo within seconds of Bo mounting it.

While Bo wasn't the greatest rodeo cowboy, he made up for it with roping.

He could rope a cow like no other man.

They acknowledged his roping skills, but Chip remained silent.

He didn't want to tell them that Bo mastered the art of roping from stealing cows off ranches when they were younger.

Bo was a fearless man. He lived a fearless life.

Chip thought about his own life. He had spent years defending the small town.

At the time outlaws outnumbered lawmen.

It was almost embarrassing, but Chip felt like he was making a difference.

Now he wondered if it was all worth it.

He couldn't shake the picture of his brother's body with the arrow in it.

For his entire life, Chip was moved by the wishes of others.

He became a lawman because his brother was such an outlaw that it broke his mother's heart.

He wanted to give her something to be proud of.

It also didn't hurt that he carried more weapons and had more training as a lawman than many his age.

He was great protection for his mother and their modest farm.

In vain, he tried to protect her from heartbreak, but he couldn't do that.

Now that he didn't have anyone to take care of, he wondered what his purpose truly would be.

Protecting his brother, keeping him out of trouble and caring for his mother were all he knew how to do.

When his mother died, he had Bo to care for.

He didn't mourn her death, because he had to travel 150 miles to the next town.

His brother had been caught stealing from the local bank and they were ready to hang him.

The day they buried his mother he was stuck arguing with a banker and spending his last dime on his brother.

It didn't help that his brother never returned any of the favors.

He had to bail his brother out of jail for theft, but his brother hopped on the horse and left without a second glance.

It was those times that he truly longed for a purpose.

Now after all of this time he suddenly felt a pang of want for a family, or someone to love him.

It seemed like everyone in his life loved him because he could do something for them.

Now he had no one to care for and no one to care for him. For the longest time he lived through his family.

He never married and never had children. At the age of 43 he doubted if it would ever happen for him.

The life of a lawman was a lonely life. He never really took any interest in anyone.

He loved the idea of being a father and a husband.

He wanted to have a family to care for. He found purpose in solving the troubles of others.

Now that he had no one to help, what was his purpose?

Chapter 15

Redd was on the tail of his last target. He couldn't wait to get the job done. He rode with a great tenacity. He tried to keep his mind on the job at hand.

His job was a simple one. This debtor didn't visit Saloons nor was he a popular person around the small town.

Redd felt a little uneasy about killing someone in front of their family, but that was Howard's request.

Apparently, this debtor was not the only person in the home who owed Howard. He was that kind of man.

The type of person to sniff out your weaknesses and use them against you. Not only was he to murder someone, he was to send a message at t he same time.

Redd smiled to himself. He didn't mind the work.

He was so anxious and ready for his money that he could barely sleep.

The spirit of Dark Eagle kept him company as he planned for the day ahead.

He spent the majority of the night, plotting and planning his next move.

His grandfather told him that he needed to be prepared for the step beyond the next step.

The next step anyone could see coming, but the step beyond catches them by surprise.

The element of surprise was his greatest asset. Surprise and the spirit of his grandfather was his secret weapon.

He prayed to his grandfather's spirit every morning and night for guidance.

As his grandfather lie on the bed dying, covered in blankets he wept.

His grandfather demanded that he not cry over him.

He asked instead that he pray with him to the ancestors that he may be allowed to guide him in the after life.

They prayed together that evening as he watched his grandfather drift off into a deep sleep.

His body shook as he felt his grandfather's spirit leave his body.

He also felt his grandfather's spirit leave his family circle. They were so deeply connected that Redd felt physical pain when his grandfather departed.

Their tribe practiced secondary bone burial. His mother mourned for days. She spent most of her time planting flowers around his gravesite and praying over it.

Redd felt horrible for his mother. A woman who knew so much sorrow should have felt a slight bit of joy.

He knew in his heart that she didn't.

It was a long honorable tradition, passed down for centuries.

They had a burial ceremony for his grandfather, and mourned for nine months. After that time, they dug him up and cleansed his bones.

After the bone cleansing and re-dedication ceremony, they buried him again.

He felt so honored to be a part of the ceremony. It seemed to seal his bond with Dark Eagle.

He continued to clean his tools as he listened to the wind blow.

The winds held the wisdom of his ancestors. They were sending him a grave warning.

Though he wasn't afraid, he made sure that he was prepared.

Chapter 16

Chip and the gang were quickly approaching Montana's mountainous terrain.

He let out a sigh of relief.

It felt like they had been riding for days. The horses were exhausted and so was he. He didn't voice a complaint, however.

He knew that complaining about the trip or the task at hand was disrespectful.

Sure the group felt like they owed it to Bo to find his killer, but he didn't want to take them for granted.

They didn't say much to each other as they continued up the hill towards the stream. They wanted to let the horses drink for a while and take another break.

Chip sighed to himself. It seemed like he was the only one in a hurry to get to Redd. He didn't voice his concern, but it was eating him up inside.

All the Grangers wanted to do was drink whiskey and rest. They weren't too keen on being pushed or encouraged, either.

Chip desperately wanted to set out on his own, but he knew in his heart that he wouldn't survive a trip like this on his own.

"Are you a man?" he asked himself as they continued to ride. No one heard his conversation with himself.

The rowdiness was so loud even the birds decided to leave. He looked up at the sky and watched the birds flee from the trees.

"How are these guys going to sneak up on a man like Redd?" he asked himself aloud.

"What kinda question you askin'" one of the Granger's demanded angrily.

He dared not repeat the question, but it appeared as if all eyes were on him. He was under the spotlight.

"You want to do this yourself?" he asked as the others joined in with the berating of the Sheriff.

"Think a man like Redd Bird is scared of a broken Sheriff?" another man asked from the crowd.

"Yeah!" they all agreed as they continued to drink their whiskey.

"He's but one man" Chip responded sounding unsure of himself. "I am but one man" he said looking around at the group of men.

Some of the men were already sleeping; their horses running wild along the pasture.

Two men were in the corner drinking themselves into a stupor and the others were berating him.

"I can do this myself" he reassured himself as he climbed on top of his horse.

The men watched him as he walked towards his horse and climbed on. They all yelled after him as his horse reared back and let out a loud noise.

They watched as Chip and Drake rode off into the dusty road, until he disappeared.

They didn't care, they continued to drink.

Chapter 17

Redd watched his target as he plowed the fields of his land. His family walked alongside of him, helping him plant for the upcoming spring season.

Redd felt a pang of guilt as he watched the man turn to his son and rub his curly head of hair.

He was skilled in archery, had been trained and practicing since he was five years old. The bow and arrow were his preferred method of execution.

Redd aimed his arrow directly at the man's back. He knew exactly where to aim to pierce through the man's heart.

He paused as he watched the man's wife walk towards him and whisper in his ear. The man walked away from the ox and plow and hugged his wife, swinging her in the air.

Redd didn't know what to think about the exchange but he was already getting bored.

The winds began to softly blow. It was his grandfather telling him that if he shouldn't hesitate.

His grandfather always told him when they were hunting, once he had the animal or target in his crosshairs he had to shoot.

There was no room for hesitation, in battle or while searching for food.

Redd put the arrow and bow in the wooden pouch on his back. He remembered the words of Howard. He had to kill the man in front of his family.

The poor man, Ernest Jester had to be shot dead, executed in front of his wife and kids.

Redd slowly walked towards Ernest and his family. They didn't notice him until he was nearly 1 foot away from them.

A great tracker, he had the ability to stealthy move across any terrain. He could go unnoticed by anyone.

This was how his people trapped and tracked animals. They had to move in silence in order to gain their prey.

When Ernest's eyes fell on Redd he let out a loud gasp. Redd leaned forward and tucked the feather in Ernest's pocket.

Ernest knew exactly what was coming next. Standing there in front of his family, his pants became wet in the front.

Redd felt terrible for the man, but he had a job to do and he was going to do it.

He tried to move his family out of the way. His wife

turned to him with a questioning look on her face.

He told her to run inside their small shack of a house. Instead, she stood there in complete shock.

The man began to plead with Redd. "Please, I can get you the money.

I have kids," he said pointing to the children, who were now surrounding their parents in a terrified hush.

Redd didn't speak, he only waited. In fact, he wasn't looking at the man or his family. His eyes were on the shack that the family lived in.

When he saw the figure move in front of the window, he let swiftly pulled out his Colt .45 and shot the man between his eyes.

By the time the body fell, Redd was on his horse, hightailing it out of town.

He could hear the wife's screams as he and Midnight trotted out of town, without a care.

As they trotted along towards Montana, he began to talk to Midnight.

"Girl, everything will be alright soon," he said as he reassured her. "We will have enough riches to return home and rebuild our land," he said as he continued bouncing along the rocky terrain.

He couldn't wait to get to Howard's ranch and snatch his money from his chubby, sweaty hands.

The wind began to gently blow behind him. He sensed that his grandfather was riding right alongside him.

They rode along into the sunset. "Next stop, freedom" he yelled as he pulled on Midnight's reigns and encouraged him to speed up.

Midnight galloped along, happily. As he felt the wind in his long braided hair, he let out a loud war cry.

Midnight followed along with a loud snort as she galloped down the road.

Chapter 18

Redd reached the Howard Manor Ranch in record speed.

He felt like a young boy again, filled with energy and ready to take on the world.

He just needed to get paid.

As he entered the ranch he noticed the field hands and cowboys watching him.

They stared at him, judging him. He smiled at them and tipped his hat.

He knew what they were thinking. They were wondering about the man dressed in traditional clothing.

He had on a full headgear and his favorite legging pants,

complete with tassels.

Midnight nuzzled his nose close to his side when he tied him to the corral. He walked towards the door of the large wooden home and knocked.

The door swung open and a beautiful caramel colored Negro woman answered the door. She had a lovely smile and delicate features.

He tipped his hat at her, "Howdy, Ma'am. Mr. Howard here" he asked as she nodded and took a step backwards.

He announced himself, "Tell'em Redd is here to see em" he said in a deep voice, hoping to impress the woman.

"Redd!" he heard from the back of the house. He walked towards the sound of the loud boisterous voice, while being accompanied by the beautiful maid.

He kept stealing glances at her. He noticed that she was

watching him. Her cheeks were red from blushing.

She walked into the great room and announced Redd to Howard and quickly walked off. Redd smiled at the fat man, wanting to kick him out of his seat.

"Job's done" he said after tipping his hat towards Howard.

He reached in his pocket and pulled out five items. A gold watch, a silver coin, a lock of hair, and two gold nuggets sat on the coffee table.

"Well" he said as he tried to stand from the chair. Redd looked at him with disgust, he looked like he had gained even more weight since he had last seen him.

"Rain?!" he yelled out his wife's name. She appeared quickly at the door, "Yes Sir?" she asked sweetly.

Redd's face lit up as he watched her beautiful face. He dared not speak to the wife of a wealthy white man like

Howard.

Instead he tried to steal glances of her in her long white dress with the pink sash. A woman walking around in white during those times, signified wealth.

She was a pure as her clothing. She looked like her hands had never done any work.

Howard cleared his throat and turned his attention back to Redd. "Get me my bag," he said not taking one eye off of Redd.

The woman looked at him for a moment too long for Redd and scurried out of the room.

"So you did the job and you pulled it off quicker than I thought," he said in a congratulatory tone. "You do great work, Redd" he said smiling.

"What are your plans after you get paid?" he asked as he watched Redd stand in front of him with an expressionless face.

Redd didn't answer him, he just continued to stare at him.

He watched as Rain ran into the room and quickly dropped the bag in the floor. She left the room as quickly as she entered.

"How much do I owe ya?" he asked as he reached into the bag that his wife sat in front of him.

Before he could remove his hands from the bag, he was dead.

Redd was holding the smoking silver encrusted, Colt 1851. The .36 caliber revolver helped him land a well-placed shot in the temple of the fat son of a bitch.

Redd moved swiftly, after he shot Howard he grabbed the back from his fat hands and peeked inside.

There was nothing inside the bag but two Smiff and Wesson shot guns. That bastard had no plans of paying him.

Redd's body was inflamed with fury. He watched as Rain came running out of the room, with a wide-eyed stare on her face.

She ran to her husband without shedding one tear. He looked at her and watched as she spit on the fat man.

"Come with me" Redd said as he grabbed the woman by her waist. She stared into Redd's dark eyes and saw deep into his soul.

Without a word they were on the back of the horse heading towards Canada.

His dreams of returning to the South would have to wait.

He was sure that he would be wanted for murder soon.

He gave the housekeeper money and told her to leave, but he knew that all of those Negros saw him enter the ranch.

One of them was bound to talk, especially with money dangled in their face.

If he was detected on the road the last place he wanted to be caught was the South.

He would be hung from the highest tree for killing a man like Howard.

As the wind blew behind him, pushing him towards the horizon he smiled.

The woman of his dreams was holding on to his waist as Midnight galloped along to safety.

Finally, his dreams were coming true.

Chapter 19

Minne walked around the small room laughing loudly as she talked to the patrons.

She excitedly slipped a dollar bill into her bra as she leaned in and kissed an old cowboy on his head.

They were playing poker and everyone was filled with whiskey and vodka. They were all feeling good.

Redd was in the bar having a drink with Midnight tied up at the corral. He felt good.

He was holding money in his pocket and had a beautiful queen on his side.

They were heading out of town, but he wanted to make sure that he came back for his money.

He buried over $10,000 behind Minnie's and he returned to get his money.

She smiled as he walked towards her. "In the back, baby" she said swinging her hefty hips in the direction that he should go.

After kissing his wife, he reassured her that he would be back. He walked towards the back of the building and opened the door.

After walking ten paces to the left he looked under the storm shelter in Ms. Minnie's back yard. Reaching for the key, he unlocked the door and slid inside the dark space.

Feeling around he found the area where he hid his lockbox. After grabbing the key from his shirt pocket, he unlocked the box.

The smell of the money hit his nostrils with the sweetest fragrance he had every smelled.

After grabbing the box, he returned the Saloon only to face Chip at the door.

"I know who you are!" he said as he charged towards Redd. Redd took two steps back with one hand on his knife, the other on his gun.

"Redd Bird?" he called out as he walked towards Redd and stood in front of him. "Ya" Redd responded as he placed his hand on his gun.

"You killed my brother" Chip called out. "Now I have to kill you" he said as he walked closer towards Redd.

"If I killed your brother it wasn't personal. If you want to make it personal. I will kill you too. I'm warning you. Walk away from here. Your brother fight is not yours, "he said growing angrier with each word.

He knew exactly who Chip was, but didn't want Chip to get himself killed.

"Walk away" he said slowly as he reached for his .45. Chip tried to be tough, but the moonlight gave him away.

He saw the tears on Chips face.

Chip shook his head and took another step forward, reaching for his gun. "I can't do that," he said as tears rolled down his face.

Before Chip could say another word, Redd shot him and Drake in the heart.

They both fell to the ground with a loud thud.

Redd returned to the inside of the Saloon and walked directly to Ms. Minnie.

He whispered in her ear that he needed a mess cleaned up.

She nodded and hollered out one name, "Virgil!" she

yelled as a un-humanly 400 pound 7 foot tall man walked towards her and leaned down.

She instructed him on what to do and he walked outside with a shovel in his hands.

"Pigs will eat anything" she said as she laughed and patted him on the back assuredly.

Redd kissed her on the cheek and slid her enough money to compensate her and Virgil. She slid the money in her bra and sashayed away towards the next customer.

Redd walked to the table and took his bride by the hand.

As the climbed on the back of Midnight and she leaned in towards his neck and whispered, "Thank you".

He squeezed her hands tightly, in a way to say, "You're welcome"

Redd knew why she thanked him. He rescued her from a life of hell. Yet, she had no idea, the life she rescued him from.

As they rode off into the sunset, Redd felt the calm wing circling around them. He smiled at the presence of his grandfather.

"Where to grandfather?" he asked as the wind grew stronger and rustled the trees to the east of him.

Midnight didn't need any more urging, he followed the directions of Dark Eagle.

Dark Eagle led them towards their destiny, his divine purpose.

Dark Eagle

"Walk tall as the trees, live strong as the mountains, be gentle as the spring winds, keep the warmth of the summer sun in your heart, and the great spirit will always be with you"

American Indian Proverb

Arise

Creek

"Be Still and the Earth will Speak to You"

- Dark Eagle

Prologue

Earl had a lot that he wanted to say to his father. "Dad, I know I'm ready to take over the business. You are getting too old to run it", he repeated to himself. Earl wasn't sure how his father would take his return. They had a huge falling out several years ago, causing Earl to flee the state in anger and fear.

After several years of living in squalor in Dodge City, Kansas he decided to return home to get what was owed to him; even if he had to take it. He rode for nearly two days thinking about what he needed to say to the old man. It was time Earl returned home and ran the business that his father owned.

He was ready to be married and needed the money and stability. His wife was used to nothing but the best and that was what she expected.

He promised to give her the best.

That was where his father came in. He needed a loan from the old man to put his little lady in a comfortable environment where they could raise their children. Being the oldest of Howard's children, he felt that he deserved it.

Riding into the hot town in a cloud of dust, Earl Howard couldn't wait to see his father. A strong, wealthy man who ruled with an iron fist, there wasn't a single person who didn't know his father, The Boss. Many people inside and on the outskirts of town knew his father. Everyone referred to him as The Boss, but Early simply called him, "Daddy".

He pulled the reins of his horse, Rider and hopped off the large horse. Brushing himself off, he took in a deep breath, grateful to be off the horse and on stable land. He cleaned his boots on the floor mat and swung the door open.

Expecting his father's young Indian squaw he stood in the foyer of the large home for a minute. She was a source of scorn for Earl. He didn't understand why his father had to take in a squaw so soon after their mother's death. It irked him. After several minutes of standing there, he called out, "Daddy", and waited to see his father's portly belly as he rounded the corner.

Instead, he was hit with a strong whiff of decay. Walking further into the house he continued yelling, calling for his daddy. When he reached the living room in the back of the home, he stopped in his tracks.

His father sat on the couch, covered in blood his vacant eyes staring at the ceiling. Screaming in fear and shock, Earl ran out of the house.

Standing outside, doubled over he coughed and vomited. Tears running down his cheeks, he tried his best not to cry, but the shock of seeing his only living parent murdered did something to him.

Once he gained his composure, Earl grew angry. His red face matched the color of his red hair. He recalled little Billie in school pointing to his hair and yelling, "Fire" at the top of his lungs. Poor Earlie was teased quite often, but his mother was always there to comfort him.

He missed her dearly and now his father was gone too. Although he didn't have a great relationship with the old bastard, he couldn't let someone kill him and get away with it. Hopping back on the horse, he grabbed the reins and forced it to rear back before galloping away.

After seeing his father slaughtered like that, bullet holes in chest, Earl's mission had changed. He was no longer a prodigal son, returning home to claim what was owed to him. He was now an orphan, ready to avenge the murder of his father.

As the horse continued to gallop away, he cried out in anger and hurt and vowed to himself that he would slit the throat of the man who murdered his dad.

Even if it killed him.

Chapter 1

"Arise", the words startled him as his eyes instantly shot open and surveyed the darkened room. He could feel his wife lying next to him, her breathing unaltered, she slept peacefully with her body close to his. He looked down at her, smiling to himself. He had his very own princess by his side.

The cold air whipped around their tent as they lay peacefully inside. "Arise", he heard the word again and sat straight up on the makeshift bed. His wife stirred an he gently patted her head telling her to go back to sleep.

As he grabbed his deerskin jacket with heavy lines of wool woven inside, by his bride, he wondered what could be calling him out of his bed so early. The sun was still hiding behind the moon. It was around 2am, he calculated by the appearance of the sky.

"My son", he heard, as he stood stoic and still. Redd Bird recognized the voice. "Yes, grandfather" he asked as he strained his ears to hear the voice of his great ancestor.

He surveyed the land beyond the mountaintop where he stood. Everything was still and quiet, as if gaining its strength for the next day.

He closed his eyes and tried to hear the voice of his ancestor again. He knew that if his mind was full and clouded with doubts and suspicions he would never hear the wisdom of Dark Eagle. "Be still and the earth will speak to you", his grandfather once shared the old proverb with him as they sat by the river one afternoon, fishing for their dinner.

Redd thought back to those days, when there was nothing on his mind aside from catching more fish than his cousins. He could sit on the riverbanks at night and hear the conversations of his elders and ancestors who walked the land centuries before him. He couldn't believe that he was so far away from his home. The thought made him uncomfortable.

"What is it grandfather", he asked as his vision began to sharpen he noticed the pitched tent in the distance. No one else would have seen it, but Redd had a gift. His grandfather called him Eagle Eye. He had the ability to seek out anything in pure darkness. His grandfather used to play games with him, making him search for the smallest items in the thick of darkness, only to laugh proudly when he returned carrying the vary item.

He didn't know at the time, but his grandfather was training him. Preparing him to seek out danger, long before it reached his home. He was hit again with a sudden pang of emptiness.

As long as Redd had been away ,he considered returning home, many times. He just didn't expect to have the sudden urge to do so. His grandfather was calling him home for a purpose.

He didn't have time to consider the purpose, however. He grabbed his bow and arrow and began making his way towards the very top of the mountain. He was wide-awake now. The voice of his grandfather had awakened him to something important.

He sat perched atop the hill, standing as quiet and stealth like a lioness seeking out their prey. Redd was an archery magician. He could hit a bull's-eye from any distance with his eyes closed. This time, however he kept his eyes wide open as he released the bow and listened to it sail through the air.

He didn't have to wait to see it hit his target. He could tell immediately that he hit the target when the arrow landed on top of the tent. Midnight was resting peacefully when Redd walked beside him and stroked his back, stirring him awake.

Before his victim bled completely out, Redd Bird and his family were on the back of Midnight, looking towards the future.

"The price of anything is the amount of life you exchange for it"

- Chief Ouray

Chapter 2

The waves crashed against Silo's feet as she played in the water, giggling with her sisters. She looked around and surveyed her property. Her family lived on this land for centuries. It was something about the land that gave her comfort, eased her twelve year old soul. She sat down and watched as her younger sisters played and danced around in the water.

It was something about their lighthearted play and laughter that suddenly made her sad. "You must", she heard the words echoing in her ears and in the wind surrounding her. "I don't want to", she cried to her mother as she was informed about her upcoming wedding to Strong Willow, their family chief.

His young wife, Shadow died during childbirth and he was searching for someone to fill the void. Eager to marry their daughter to the wealthiest, most powerful person in the their Tribal town, parents lined up for miles, lobbying with the great chief.

Each family in their 2,000-member Tribal town brought

gifts and bribes to the chief in an effort to win favor. She shook her head in pity watching her parents hurry off after the others. She knew that if they won his affections, she would have to leave her four sisters and her family, forever.

Shadow wasn't much older than her. A deep shiver ran through her spine as she considered her own fate. What if she were to end up the same way, buried in a pine box in the honorable grave fields, at the age of twelve.

She had to shake her head to loosen the thoughts clouding her mind.

"Silo" her sister were calling to her to join them in their play. They had no idea about the conversation she had with her parents earlier that morning. They didn't know that she was no longer a child, but a woman about to be married.

The Chief had four wives, but as a chief he could marry as many as he wanted. Every few years, he grew tired of his previous wife or she worked herself to death and he would replace her with a new one.

She despised the process, but what could she do?

Her mother was in their tiny home, lovingly sewing her daughter's wedding garments for the ceremony. It had all been decided long before they sat Silo down for the conversation. "You will be wed in several days", her father said as he proudly pat his daughter on the head. "The Chief is anxious to marry you. You have brought great honor to our family", he said as his daughter tried her hardest not to cry.

She waited until her parents were sound asleep and cautiously left their tent. The black night sky was littered by bright bursts of light. She loved watching the sky at night. The moon accompanied the stars, casting a lovely glow on her home.

"What can I do", she wondered aloud. She wished that Raising Sun was around to console her. Raising Sun was her great grandmother and she was the wisest woman Silo knew. Although she respected her mother and her grandmother, neither had the compassion or the wisdom of Raising Sun.

As she sat on the wet grass she stared at the sky and whispered, "Raising Sun" to the emptiness. She knew that her attempt was futile. Her great grandmother was now a spirit, raised months ago to join her beloved husband in the sky.

The wind began to softly blow as Silo sat completely still, allowing the air to lift her hair as it blew. She felt her great-grandmother's presence in the wind. She could smell her incense and instinctively smiled at the familiar scent.

When Silo arose an hour later she realized that the wind had put her into a deep sleep, she couldn't have been more grateful for her great-grandmother's presence. It was in that visit that she knew exactly what she had to do.

Silo had her mind made up. Staring at the Tribal town one last time, she wipe away a single tear as she slipped away from the Tribal town on foot to her new destiny.

Chapter 3

Rex chomped on his cigar as he surveyed the crowded Saloon. Mr. Leven was as loud as ever, talking about his lazy, do for nothing children. "All they do is eat and crap", he complained, taking a long swig out of the mug. "You know, ain't no use havin' money when yo chirren hate ya", he said with tears in his eyes, raising the glass to the bartender for a refill.

Rex wiped at his wet brow trying to decide if he should stop the bartender from giving the old man more. Mr. Leven was one of their regulars, heck he kept the entire Saloon running off his beer tab alone.

After several drinks he always found himself sitting at the bar with his head in his hands, begging the waitresses to go home with him. Some of them did, too. He would hear of the stories through his Beth Anne. She was the head waitress in the bar and made sure the others stayed in line.

She told Rex that Mr. Leven lived like a pauper when he had gold coins simply lying about as if they were nothing.

He offered the money to Beth Anne once. She followed him home one night after he was too drunk to walk by himself. She helped him into his carriage and inside his house. She claimed that she refused his offer after he begged and pleaded with her to stay the night for $150.

Rex wasn't sure he believed that though, Beth Anne was a bit of a harlot. She went home with some of her best customers, simply because of a nice tip.

He watched as the loud man in front of him took a long swig of his beer and grabbed ahold of one of the waitresses. "Come here honey", he said as he tried to kiss the repulsed young lady.

Rex was growing tired of some of his patrons, but he didn't know what to do. He glared at the man, imagining himself shooting him in the middle of the street. Rex could literally see the man's lifeless body collapse to the ground.

Carter owed the Saloon nearly a thousand dollars, which was a pretty high tab. In other parts of the country, Carter would have been dead the moment he entered the bar.

Rex wanted to do it; he had to do it, but he couldn't. He was a business owner; his father bequeathed the Saloon to him over a decade ago when he passed away under the hot Oregon sun. Along with the dusty Saloon, he also owned a fifteen-acre farm and several horses.

Rex was a wealthy man, by all accounts. He was also a coward.

The doors swung open and in walked a tall young man, with skin the color of copper. It was something about this man that gave Rex the chills. The way he surveyed the Saloon with a regal presence, showed that he was of Indian descent. The man walked towards the front of the bar where Rex stood, wiping down the counter top with an old sour rag.

"Howdy", he said as the man responded with a tip of the hat.

Rex grew uncomfortable under the man's glare. He didn't say a word, he just stood in front of the bar and looked around slowly. When his gaze locked onto that of another patron, the young man tipped his hat again, knowingly.

He then straightened his hat and walked out of the bar.

The man that was laughing loudly had been silenced as everyone watched the door, long after the man left. Rex wondered about the man who came into the bar and silenced his worst customer with just a look.

Rex watched as Carter wiped sweat away from his brow and stood slowly, checking his side holsters for his pistols. Rex's heart pounded against his chest as he envisioned the man shooting him as opposed to settling his hefty tab. Instead the man walked towards the door of the Saloon and slowly sauntered outside.

Rex listened as the swinging door to his Saloon swung open then closed suddenly, with a loud thud. Rex was shocked, for once he could literally hear the door close. The entire bar was quiet by now, everyone silently wondering what was going to happen next.

They didn't have to wonder for long, however.

The sound of one-shot gun blast tore through the air as everyone in the Saloon ran to the window to see what happened.

Rex couldn't believe it. He rubbed his eyes twice and stared in shock as the patrons in the building began to talk excitedly. "What was that?", the wondered aloud.

Carter was lying on his back with a hole in his chest. Rex strained his eyes to see in the distance the tall man riding on a black horse, dust standing up.

"Did you see that", the waitress asked as she walked behind Rex with a shocked expression on her face. "Yes, who was that man", he wondered as the room grew quiet.

"That was Redd Bird. The deadliest man in the West",

the short man who was seated at the bar said as he slowly stood to leave. At the sound of the name, several other patrons stood and left the Saloon.

He stared out the old dusty window in his Saloon, long after Redd Bird was gone. "Redd Bird", he murmed under his breath. This Indian man would be the answer to all of his problems.

"Beth", he called out to the waitress circling the floors, looking for plates and mugs to clear. "What", she called out with a hint of annoyance. No one could tolerate Rex and recently he was becoming unbearable to be around. He thought everyone was out to get him and his dusty Saloon. Folks talked about him and his place with disgust.

Rex was a child when he inherited the Saloon and the workers. 16 years old and he had the nerve to try and tell them what to do. She wanted to throw something at him, instead she swung around and smiled. "I mean, what can I help you with", she asked with a syrupy tongue.

"I need to get word to Redd Bird", he said casually as she brushed him off. He had no idea what he was getting himself into.

"Suga, I'm not sure if that's the tree you want to go barking up", she said as she tossed her bright red curls and walked towards the patron beckoning for her, leaving Rex with his own thoughts.

Chapter 4

"Forty….fifty…sixty", Caesar counted as he made a tremendous show of the money he counted before Redd. Caesar was a tall man with fire red hair and a thin frame. He looked like he could slide between the bars of any jail cell created for a man. Redd nearly chuckled as he watched the man, imagining him slipping through jail cell bars.

He smiled to himself as the man finished counting. "Thank you", Redd Bird said as he stared at the man long and hard, then turned to walk out of the room. "Hold on for a moment", Caesar called behind him. Redd knew that Caesar had another target for him. He always did.

Redd never trouble making money. The evil of man would keep him employed forever. He turned around and faced Caesar with a strong stare. He wanted the man to know that he wasn't playing around with him.

Everyone knew what Redd Bird did to his previous employer; killing the man and snatching his bride. Redd didn't care, in fact he loved it.

As long as everyone feared him, he was in business. No one really cared for his previous employer anyway. Redd Bird's only regret was that he didn't get paid for killing the sorry sap.

"I have someone..", he said allowing his voice to trail, hoping that Redd would beg for more information. He hoped wrong. Redd stood there counting the seconds. His grandfather told him to be a patient man, but not too patient. He must allow his own will to carry him, not the lure of temptation.

He began to walk towards the door when the man spoke quickly, "I need you to go after another person. He owes me nearly $1,000", Caesar said hoping that it would entice Redd to at least smile or smirk. Instead, Redd Bird stood there waiting for the rest.

"Here", he said tossing a newspaper at Redd Bird. "I need you to kill him", Caesar added. "I don't want the money anymore. Any man who owes me longer than a month, doesn't owe me money. He owes me his life", he said in a deadly tone.

Redd Bird walked out of the room. "Will you take it", he called out, knowing that Redd Bird was on his way to his next target.

"Hold on to what is good…even if it is a handful of the earth"

- Green Moss

Chapter 5

Awakened by the sun Silo let out a deep breath and looked around. Her surroundings were as vast as the land she recently left. She already missed her home, the smell of the jasmine and fresh herbs permeating throughout the entire land. She could hear her sisters laughing and playing in the river as if they had no worries in the world.

Her head was pounding like the beat of the Penobscot drums, beckoning her to return home, but her heart said something different. Silo felt an aching loneliness settle deep within her, but she wouldn't give in to it.

She simply gave thanks for arising and looked towards the sky, where the ancient spirits of her ancestors resided. "Give me the eyes to see and the strength to understand", she said as she took in the fragrant earth. She would head towards the west. There would be plenty of work for her. She was an excellent cattle herder.

She gathered her things and put them inside the leather sack her mother gave her when she was only five. "For life's unknown journeys", she whispered as she handed it to her baby girl at her birthday celebration.

Four hours later Silo stopped and wiped the sweat from her sun burned face. She was exhausted, but she continued to walk. She had plenty of water in her canteen and plenty of energy in her body, but she knew that she had to do better.

That was when she noticed the camp ahead. A beautiful brown stallion was tied to a post in the ground. Silently, she watched the haggard looking pale faced man eating out of a bowl, staring at the sky. She shook her head as the thoughts began to circle.

"This is your horse", she heard the voice say as she nodded in agreement. The stallion would take her where she needed to go, but first she had to separate the beautiful creature from his owner.

Slowly removing the bow and arrow from her bag, she watched as the man cleaned his dishes in the nearby river. He looked like he had been out there for a long time. She felt sorry for him. Silo was the best marksman in the Tribal town. She knew that it would take nothing to kill the man, but something stopped her.

There had to be another way...

She looked at the sky, searching for an answer. The last thing she wanted to do was kill someone, especially her first day out of their Tribal town. She thought of different scenarios as darkness fell upon them.

Lying in the makeshift bed, she stared at the sky. It held no answers for her. Silo knew that when her ancestors were silent, she was to be still. She closed her eyes and allowed the darkness to overtake her.

The sound of footsteps in the distance woke her from her sleep. She wiped at her eyes and turned her attention to the direction of the footsteps. Someone was preying upon her, and whoever it was they were not very good about it. Slowly, she reached into her bag and pulled out the bow and arrow.

Closing one eye she aimed for the target in the thick wooded area behind her. She heard the thud and began to walk towards it, hoping that it was an animal. She was hungry and hadn't eaten more than the things she hastily grabbed as she ran from her childhood home.

Now her stomach was growling, reminding her that she needed to fill it with nourishment before heading out. Counting her footsteps, she remembered where the sound came from. She walked in the direction of the wailing animal.

When she approached it, she grabbed it with both arms and pulled it out into the moonlight. She gasped when she saw the pale face of a man. "Help me", he called to her as he tried to remove the arrow from chest. "Are you alone", she inquired, hoping that he had the strength to respond.

"Yes, help", he said trying to reach for her. Silo stared at the helpless man in silence. She knew that it wouldn't be long before the poison would enter the man's heart, causing it to stop.

Silo watched as the man twisted and turned in agony before she saw the life finally leave his eyes. Saying a prayer she dragged the man back into the woods and let the animals have their way with him as she packed her things and began walking towards his camp, with only the moon to light her path.

Silo was disappointed that she didn't feel sadness for the man who she killed. She told herself that she was only protecting herself, but something inside of her told her different.

She was no longer young Silo. She was now an outlaw and she loved the way that sounded.

"We are all of one fire"

- Creek Nation

Chapter 6

"Where will we live", his bride asked with real concern etched on her face. Redd Bird smiled at the woman and responded, "I will take care of you and our child", he said as he gently rubbed her swollen stomach. He couldn't help but wish that he was back in their Tribal town, raising his family.

The dusty, deadly wild west was not a place to raise a child and he knew it, but what else could he do? Redd Bird was not the type of man that could work a regular job. He was not just a cowboy or a farm hand, he was an assassin.

The word alone gave him great pride, but he was now a husband and a father. His bride would be having a baby soon and he had to make sure that they were taken care of.

It was time for him to settle down. He looked at his bride as she hastily prepared their dinner. They would be eating fresh salmon from the nearby springs. He enjoyed fresh fish and his bride knew it. Since the day he rescued her she had been appreciative and supportive. He didn't have to request a meal, it was already cooking when he returned from a job. His most recent job, he left her home, resting peacefully.

He hated leaving her alone.

The west was not a proper place for a woman to live alone. All types of outlaws and fugitives ravaged the area. He couldn't help but think of her as he rode away quickly from his last kill.

He despised the vulnerability that came along with being a married man. How could he be a father? He was already vulnerable with a wife. If the wrong person found out about his family, they would hurt them to get to him and he couldn't have that.

Redd couldn't leave his wife in their Tribal town either. She demanded to be by his side. That was her only request, that he never leave her to sleep alone. She was afraid of living out in the open. She didn't understand the pleasures that came with living on your own.

Solitude was something that Redd Bird craved. When he first left the tribal town in the south, he hurt and longed for companionship, until he learned to love his alone time.

Catē changed everything.

She also didn't understand how lethal Redd Bird was. He didn't take kindly to feeling weak. His bride added a level of weakness that Redd Bird couldn't understand. As he watched her carefully remove the fish from the fire, he couldn't help but thank the ancestors for her.

A Sioux woman, she didn't quite understand the ways of the Creeks but she wanted to learn. He smiled as he heard her humming one of their Mvskoke hymns.

His wife whom he affectionately called, "Catē" which meant red in Hitchiti, his native language. He felt the name was fitting. She had a red hot temper and a fire within her that would not burn out. That was the reason for his attraction to her. He vowed to never refer to her as Howard did. The moment she left that old sloppy bastard's house, she left behind the name Rain and everything associated with it.

It wasn't about the physical, Redd Bird wanted something substantial. He had plenty of women. He wanted a woman who would love him the way his father loved his mother. Catē was turning out to be a great helper and companion for him. Most importantly, she was willing to be taught.

That made him happy.

His people were spread throughout the Southeastern part of the vast land. There were many tribes of the Creek nation, but they were all one people with one love and one heartbeat.

He knew that his people were spread out. Redd no longer had parents living in the tribal town so he felt like there was no point in returning. When he noticed his wife's growing belly, he let out a sigh.

It was time to head back south. His wife needed to be in a peaceful place before she gave birth to his seed. He yearned to raise his child on the same land in which he was raised.

He stared at the bow and arrow lying casually against their tent, begging for attention.

He just had one thing left to do.

Chapter 7

With the moonlight shining the way, Silo walked carefully approaching the camp of the man she killed. She didn't have time to reflect on death.

Her hearing was impeccable. She cleared her mind, closed her eyes and opened her ears. She needed to check to see if the man she killed the night before had a companion with him.

After a while she hurried into the woods and noticed the man lying on the ground with an arrow in his chest. As she placed her foot on his stomach, she pulled on her arrow until it finally loosened.

She said a silent prayer over the man's wounded body and began her trek towards the man's horse and camp. It didn't take Silo long to reach the abandoned camp. She held on to her bow and arrow as she approached the deceased man's camp area.

She opened the tent as she held her breath. What would she do if someone were in the camp? She let the breath out when she realized that the camp ground was empty. She looked around at the forest lurking behind the tent and put her keen sight to the test. Satisfied that no one was around, she began to search the camp for food.

When she found fresh vegetables she reached for them, giving thanks first she bit into the apple that was in the man's sack. As she snacked on the apple, she stared at the horse, tied up behind the camp. She had given him some of the vegetables that she located in the camp ground and he was chewing happily without a care in the world.

Silo was not afraid of a horse, even one as large as the stallion in front of her. She had to break in new horses on the farm and had no fear in her heart when she approached the horse again.

He made a few noises as she gently stroked his muscled shoulders and ran her hands to his nose. He looked at her with eager eyes. "You belong to me", she whispered to him as the horse snorted and kicked his feet in the air.

She rubbed the horse, gently.

"You belong to me", she whispered as he finally began to settle. She looked around and located a worn and weathered saddle which she threw on the back of the horse along with the few things she took when she left their tribal town as she and her new horse rode off into the sunset.

She let out a loud yell, which made the horse go even faster. She loved it. The wind was blowing and all she could see ahead of her was the wide open world ahead. Her newfound freedom was awaiting her, she couldn't turn back the other way.

She couldn't stop the images of the man lying on his back with the hole in his heart. She smiled to herself as the images replayed themselves. If she were at home, she would have received a white feather with a black tip. The tribe would have come together and hosted a feast that would last for days.

She touched the feathers on her traditional headdress as she recalled the memories that made her home so sweet. She killed her first person at the age of 12. She was so proud of herself.

It was a man lurking around their tribe from a neighboring town. She snuck up on the man and took his scalp. Her father was so proud of her, he let her sleep for hours after the morning horn sounded.

"I will make you proud again", she said aloud as she and her new horse rode off as the sun rose high above her head, searching for an adventure.

Chapter 8

Rex surveyed the bar and slipped away to the back of the building. The music and the loud talking were making him lightheaded. He swung open the door to his office, pushing past to waitresses talking in the hall, "Back to work", he called out to them slapping one of them on the behind.

His office was in shambles. He pushed all of the papers and lien notices aside and plopped down in the seat. He was nearly $3,000 dollars in debt and he knew that he had to act fast.

The loans were due to his inability to stay out of the bottom of an whisky bottle. The Saloon wasn't the only thing that was passed down throughout generations. His father died an old drunk and so did his grandfather. They both were dead before 60.

His father didn't die a natural death, though. He recalled his father stumbling into the house late one night and slapping his mother around. It was something that he and his older brother Carl knew all too well. It all happened the same, but something was different that night. Rex could smell death in the air and he was terrified. Rex could hardly sleep that night. He lay away, praying that it wouldn't happen.

Hours earlier, his brother confided a secret. "I'm going to kill daddy tonight", he said nonchalantly as if he were telling him that he was sneaking down to the local Saloon for a beer after work. His older brother was a tall boy with dark features and dark curly hair.

At age 15 he was already taller than their father and stronger. Rex watched him wrestle with a man at the Saloon who came to the house looking for their father. Carl senior had a habit of betting and losing to the wrong people.

Those people always found themselves at their door in the middle of the night, searching for their money. His poor mother begged them for mercy. She didn't know anything about the money her husband owed.

One man, Phill Sullian didn't appreciate being turned

away. He yelled at their mother and raised his hand to slap her. His brother put him on the ground so quickly, Rex didn't have a chance to move. He knew that his brother was strong.

"How are you going to do that", Rex asked his brother terrified of the answer. "Just wait and see", he said as he tossed a bale full of hay on the pickup truck bed. "Haul ass boys", his father was yelling from his seated position on the porch. Rex didn't know how to stop his brother, even if he wanted to. He didn't want to stop him.

Something deep inside of Rex was blood thirst enough to do the deed himself.

Chapter 9

Hours turned into days, Silo felt like she had been riding forever. Dusk had quickly fallen over the vast land. After noticing an area thick with trees she decided it was time they stopped for a rest. When she pulled on the reins of the horse and leaned back, the horse began to slow.

She hopped off the back of the horse and grabbed the reins in her hands; walking her horse towards the thick brush. Once her feet hit the ground she realized that they had been riding for too long. Silo decided that this would be the area where she pitched her tent. She needed to be away from the road and off in an area where no one could easily happen upon them.

Reading the compass and map she held tightly in her hand, Silo let out a sigh. She and her new friend, Sheba were resting at the seat of a large Elm tree. She tried to determine what direction she wanted to go, but was torn. She recalled the stories Running Panther told about the Creek tribal town in the Northeast area of the country.

Silo thought about heading north, but she couldn't turn herself in that direction. There was nothing for her there. She couldn't live free, there. The moment she stepped foot off her family land she knew that she could never return to the traditional.

As her grandmother once told her, she was like a fire; burning through anything that crossed its path. Fire had the strength to take down anything and yet things are still born through fire.

She was as complex as the definition of her true name, Fire Moss. She smiled at the memory of her grandmother and the home she left behind.

After she stood and brushed the dirt off, she motioned towards the water bucket, urging the horse to finish drinking. "We have a long road ahead of us", she said trying to convince the stubborn horse. She watched as he took a step forward and continued lapping the water.

Silo made the decision to head west. She was heading in the direction anyway. There was no point in hustling towards the North only to find herself married to a man three decades older than her.

The vision of her mother trying to convince her to marry that old man made her want to vomit. She couldn't believe her family thought it made sense for her to live a life like that. She was proud of herself for making the decision to leave, but she felt terrible about leaving her mother alone.

She was the oldest child. Silo was the oldest of their children and the one they looked to. Now there was no one to walk her sisters to the river and retrieve the fish baskets, to help the girls search for vegetables and tend to their gardens.

Chapter 10

Rex was fast asleep when the knock came to his door. He didn't know who would be bothering him so late, but he planned to find out. Grabbing his shotgun, Rex approached his front door with caution. "Who is it", he called out with the gun aimed at the offender.

"Get that damn gun away from me", the short man said staring down the barrel of the gun without fear. Rex shuddered at the sight of the little man. Lance Mitchell was a name that many feared. He was the only man who carried out his own hits.

Lance was less than five feet tall and had a temper which racked up bodies clear across the country. He was the man that no one wanted to be on the bad side of. Rex however, found himself on the bad side of Lance and he hated his position.

"Come in, sir", he said reaching for the man's hat only to be slapped away. "I don't want to intrude on anything", he said never taking his eyes away from Rex's. "I am here on business", he said answering Rex's question. "Do you have my money", he demanded, his once calm face twisting into that of a red faced, angry devil. Rex shook with fear, angry with himself about being afraid of a man with such small stature.

"I only have half of your money, sir. I promise I'll have the rest in a month", he said pleading with the man, shaking from the sudden chill that cut through to his underwear. Suddenly, he was very aware that he was standing outside in his drawers.

"I will give you two weeks", the man said pushing Rex in his chest. Rex fell against the wall, surprised by the brute force of a little person.

"But…", before Rex had an opportunity to respond the man pulled out a .45 and put it to Rex's temple. "If you don't have my money when I return, you will not have a chance to explain", he said turning on his heels.

Rex slammed the door shut and turned to face his trembling wife, "What's going on, Rex", she demanded with her hands on her hips. "Woman don't question me", he responded to the startled woman.

Rex knew that he had to find a way to get ahold of some money and fast. He had to collect on the debts owed to him. Rex scratched his balding head until it was sore. If he didn't get his money back in two weeks, he and his wife would be dead.

What was he going to do. He couldn't tell his wife that they had less than a month to live on this lovely earth. Instead, he had to come up with a plan. A plan to save their lives and grab ahold of money.

His wife watched him as he returned to bed, in shock. Rex would have explained it all to his wife, if Lance hadn't taken his breath away. The man could hardly speak.

Chapter 11

Redd Bird pulled out his .45 and walked towards the trembling man. "H....how much did he pay", the man stuttered, begging for his life. He knew who took the hit out against him. Everyone knew when they were experiencing consequences of their wrongs, they just didn't want to be faced with it.

"I said I'll pay anything", the man repeated as Redd Bird sent the hot slug through his chest, watching the man fall to the ground.

He hopped on his horse and left as the towns folk gathered around the man, pointing after him. Redd Bird never stayed long enough to answer questions or to be seen. He completed the job like a professional.

His bride was at the camp that he setup for them a few days ago. They were a nomadic set of people; never staying in one place longer than a few days. His bride didn't have a problem with their lifestyle. She simply fathered their things and prepared to leave again.

He wanted to purchase a coach for her and another horse but that would require that they be stationary and he wasn't sure if they were ready for that. Redd Bird still had ground to cover.

He wanted to eventually head to the south. Redd Bird decided that north would be the best place to raise his family. Redd wanted to head north at that moment, but he knew that he had to make more money; secure more funds. Running wouldn't do him or his family any good. He looked at the paper that his new employer handed him.

He couldn't stand Caesar any more than he could his previous boss, but Caesar was a fair man. Redd Bird pulled out the gold coins that Caesar tossed to him after handing him the paper with the names on it.

He absently counted the coins, thinking about the things that he needed to purchase with the money, blood money. Blood was spilled over every coin he received from Caesar. He recounted the coins and considered Caesar's smiling face as he counted the money out to him.

"The other half when you get back", he said smiling, with his bright red hair standing on top of his head as if it were on fire.

There were five names on the list; three more to go. He wanted to finish his job and collect the remaining half of his money and pay for his to give birth in the warm temperatures of the south.

Chapter 12

"What you doing out here by yourself, little lady", she heard the voice and jumped. She didn't hear the man creep upon her. The man that stood over her was rough looking with a long, dirty beard. His eyes were squinted as if he were looking into the sun.

She didn't respond.

Suddenly, she felt the slap across her face. She jumped out poised to fight, only to be knocked back down. The man assaulted her for what seemed like hours, though she was sure it wasn't that long.

As she tasted blood in her mouth, she gritted her teeth; reaching for her bag. If she could just get to her bag she would give this man something he never would be able to forget.

She kicked herself for falling asleep so soundly. She knew better. The man stood over the young girl, straddling her as he continued to beat on her. When he finally stopped he reached for her dress. Silo knew exactly what the man's intentions were. She kicked and screamed, trying to avoid the inevitable assault.

She knew exactly what was on the man's mind. She could see it in his eyes. The moment he leaned in close to her face, she reacted.

Since he had her arms and her legs pinned, she knew that there was only one thing to do. She lunged forward and bit down as hard as she could on his jugular. Silo didn't let up until she tasted the man's blood in her mouth. He reeled back in pain, squealing like a little pig.

While he took the time to recover, she reached for her knife. The only knife that she ever held. She hurled the knife in the man's chest and twisted it, ensuring that the man would die from his wounds.

Spitting on the man in disgust she continued to stab him until she was sure that he would no longer move. Nursing her wounds, Silo continued to spit blood from her mouth.

She didn't have the time to cry over her situation. Silo had to get out of the area, quickly. She wasn't sure if someone would come looking for the dead creature lying on the floor of her tent.

Checking his pockets for change, she had a little solace with the fact that her attacker had money on him. Sinking the change in her satchel she hastily gathered her things from her camp.

The disgusting creature that lie dead only a few inches away from her taught her something that night. He taught her to watch her own back. Silo never experienced anything like what that man was trying to do to her and she vowed to never experience it again.

Wiping the man's blood on his dirty shirt, she cleaned her knife. The knife felt heavy in her hand. The handle was carved from pure ivory with the initials of her great grandmother etched in the handle. Handed down from multiple generations, Silo recalled the day her mother placed the knife in her hands.

"Treat it well", she whispered as she looked over her

shoulder to ensure that her husband wasn't near. "This knife is a secret, given to me from my mother and her mother before her, this knife has brought us luck and safety", she said smiling proudly at her daughter.

"Be careful not to let your husband see this", she said as Silo nodded in pride. Her mother gave her the knife days before her wedding. She was so proud of her daughter, marrying the Chief of their tribal town.

Silo shook her head, erasing the memories of her mother's smile. She knew that her mother would be worried about her, but she didn't have time to think about that. She could only move forward.

As the moon lit her way, she decided at that moment that her family no longer existed. She was a lone woman, taking the world on by herself. In this world there was no room for family or feelings.

That night, Silo retained her dignity but lost her innocence.

Chapter 13

When the sun rose high in the sky, Rex was already at work sifting through his receipts and notes. He had to look for the names of everyone who owed him money.

He raked his through his thick tuft of hair on his head, scratching at his scalp. Rex couldn't believe it. He knew that he had bar tabs and bills for everyone in the bar, yet he couldn't find one single name.

He was searching for names to give to Redd Bird once he located him. His special visitor the previous night gave Rex enough initiative to make up his mind. After Lance left his home, he stayed wide awake in the bed. He tried to comfort his wife, telling her that everything was okay. Rex knew he was lying.

If he didn't get the other half of his money to Lance, he and his wife were in danger.

"Morn'n suga", Beth Anne said as she walked into the

bar, startling Rex. He jumped up from his seat and ran to the door, locking it behind them.

Beth stared at him with her mouth hanging wide open. "Suga is everything okay", she asked as Rex sat down, wiping sweat from his brow with an old rag he kept in his pocket.

"Suga", Beth said as she placed her hand on Rex's shoulder. "Everything is fine, Beth Anne", he said motioning with his hand for her to leave him alone. "Rex, what's gotten into you", she asked, not paying his gesture the bit of attention.

He didn't respond. He could only stare at the wall in front of him. On the wall was a picture of the Saloon when he first inherited it. He stood outside of the building with a big smile on his face, appearing ready for the world.

If only he would have simply walked away from it all, just like he planned. His brother had been dead for nearly a decade when he inherited the Saloon.

With his head in his hands, he began to weep thinking about the last time he saw his brother. He was smiling at his young brother, boasting and proud to have killed their father.

The moment his mother began screaming, Carl swung into action. He pulled out the large knife that they used to hack down tall bushes on the farm and used it chop off his father's head.

His mother screamed like never before. He thought she would never stop screaming. Rex covered his ears in fear. He didn't know what would happen. In his youthful ignorance he expected his father to stand up and lunge at them with his hands outstretched. Instead, his father lay in a puddle of his own blood, his head on one side of the room, his body on the other.

Then he heard a voice that he never heard before. "Leave this house", was all he heard as Rex and his brother stared at their mother in stunned silence. "You killed my husband", she screamed as she tried to kill her own son, her savior; the person who saved her from endless whoopings was now avenging her husband's murder.

"Get out or I will shoot", she said grabbing the rifle and aiming it at a terrified Carl. Rex didn't hear his brother speak a word, before he opened the door and backed out of the house, still staring at his mother in shock.

"If you stay here, the law will get you", she said motioning with the gun for him to leave. "Get", she said as Carl waved a sad, final "goodbye" to his brother.

Rex didn't see his mother cry until the day she received word that her oldest son was found stealing food from a farmer three towns over. He was hanged for his crime. Carl, dead at the age of 18. In Rex's twisted world, his brother was killed by his father and he always believed that.

His mother never said a word about his brother or his father again. She forbid him and his brother from speaking of them as well. She claimed that it was no sense in thinking about the dead, they couldn't do anything about it and neither could she.

His mother died of a broken heart less than three years after that, leaving the Saloon, the house and nothing but sadness behind.

Rex began to weep as Beth Anne stared at him in a shocked silence.

Chapter 14

Redd Bird and his bride rode along the worn, dust road searching for his next target. He loved visiting this area of the west. He could almost smell Miss Minnie's cooking from a mile away. He told himself that he wouldn't return to this town, but money was there and he followed the trail of money.

His bride was holding on to him as tight as she could. He knew what she was thinking. Redd could literally read her mind.

"We have to return here", he said nonchalantly answering her question. "Don't worry, I have no problems taking care of us both", he said patting her on the shoulder.

She let out a reassured sigh, but he knew that her mind was churning with lethal possibilities. His was too.

She pleaded with him to show her how to handle the

rifle. At first he brushed the idea aside. The last thing he wanted her to deal with was protecting them both, especially with her now pregnant, swollen belly.

The sun was slowly rising over the sleepy town. Redd Bird knew that he had a name for himself. He was an assassin, of course plenty of unsolved murders were added to his docket.

He didn't care about that.

All Redd Bird cared about was protecting his family and securing enough money to keep them fed and safe. He slowed the horse down to a trot and veered the reins towards the tree lined area surrounding the worn road.

He knew that his bride's head was filled with questions. Without saying a word, he thrust the weapon in her hand and waited to see what she would do.

Redd Bird stood in shock as he watched his dainty bride, cock the machine and shoot at the tree that was sitting in front of them. He laughed to himself as she smiled in pride. "Who taught you to shoot", he asked as she fell back in his arms laughing. "I observe everything with my eyes, heart and mind", she simply replied as she climbed on the horse and waited for him to climb back on.

He couldn't believe it, someone was able to outsmart him or at least shock him. That was not a usual thing. In fact, if the woman had not been his beloved bride he would have killed her right where she stood.

Redd didn't take too kind to surprises.

Redd Bird placed the rifle back inside the satchel and hopped on the horse without saying a word. He simply smiled to himself. His bride was prepared for battle, even if he didn't want her involved in it.

The wind was now at their back, pushing them onward. He knew that his grandfather was urging him to finish his tasks and then take his bride back to their home. "Yes, grandfather", he said as a response to the wind which now circulated around them. Redd was always obedient to the wind and the call of his grandfather.

Overhead he heard the squeal of an eagle signaling that he was on the right path to his blessed future.

That was all Redd Bird needed. "Yah", he called out as he slapped the reins of the horse and Midnight reared back loudly, only to land on his feet and push onward.

Chapter 15

Silo and her friend sat atop a tall hill overlooking the town below. She could see smoke from the fires that were burned around the outskirts of the dusty town. She smiled to herself, pleased that she reached the west. There was much to do inside this town, if she planned to remain alive.

She watched with a keen eye as the townsfolk went about their day. The women dressed in their frilly gowns and the men with their tall hats and their loud boots echoing from the wood floors.

She continued to watch until she was satisfied.

Silo didn't look away until she noticed the activity surrounding one stagecoach. People walked around the tiny horse drawn coach carrying bags of loot and they left the stagecoach with nothing.

Silo kept her eyes on the building and the people walking

around the stagecoach.

She made up her mind. Silo needed money to continue living her life of freedom. This building was holding the only link between her and her freedom.

She had a plan devised and she would be successful. As she looked at the money in her hand and thought about the attack from the previous night she made up her mind.

The time had come for Silo to prove that she had what it took to survive alone in the wilderness. She laughed to herself as she recalled her first "adult" test.

She had to spend the week in the thick of the forests surrounding their home. Silo was given the responsibility of bringing back a wild boar from her time in the woods.

She remembered the tears that welled up in her mother's eyes as she watched her first born leave their hut. She also recalled the look of sheer pride on her father's face when they feasted for nearly a month on the meat from the two boars she returned with.

"You have the spirit of a wolf", her father said as he chewed the delicious meat. Her grandmother sat in silence. After their feast they had a ceremony where young Silo was named. Her grandmother was tasked with naming the children in the community. She had a deep connection with the ancestors.

She had no problem with what she planned to do. She knew that sometimes she had to do what she didn't want to do to survive. That didn't bother Silo, this was what she now lived her life by.

Once darkness fell Silo went into action. She traced the path of the stagecoach, preying on it like a panther. She watched as the wagon bumped along the road without a care. Once the wagon made its way along her path she sprung into action.

Stumbling out of the darkness wearing only her torn top and her bruises from the other nights encounters, Silo was a sight to behold. The driver of the stagecoach pulled on the reins, halting the vehicle to a complete stop and stared in shock at the young girl. She knew he couldn't understand him and he couldn't understand her, but she saw the look in his eye and she used that weakness against him.

Aiming the weapon at the man, she motioned for him to get out of the seat. He began to mumble something in a language she had trouble discerning. She stood there for a while, watching as he tried to raise the reins to get the horses moving.

Unfazed by his movements, Silo aimed the rifle towards the ground where the startled man stood and fired.

When she rifle fired, he began to jump and finally he moved out of the stagecoach and stood on the dusty ground. Certain things were universal in all languages. Once he climbed out of the stage coach she peaked inside and stared in awe at the loot. She stole food, water and plenty of coins to ensure that her pockets remained full for days.

She felt sorry for the man, standing out in the middle of

the Arizona dessert in his undergarments. She also felt another stronger emotion, pride. Silo knew that there was no turning back.

Robbing stagecoaches was her new job and she was a professional at it.

Chapter 16

Nightfall came and Rex was still sitting in his office staring at his desk. Resting on the top of his desk was a bill from Lance. Five years prior, Rex was an excited twenty something ready for the world. His mother had passed away and his surviving siblings ran from the tiny, dusty Arizona town the moment they laid their mother to rest.

She was the glue that held them all together. Although, they all blamed their mother for their brother's death, they still stayed in the small house that their father built with his hands.

Rex and his younger brother Clyde were responsible for tending the tiny garden and the farm animals, trying to survive. They were a poor family, but rich in love. The entire town was very poor.

That was their purpose. All of them. They were so poor and with the Saloon being run by his uncles, whom his mother was convinced were stealing money from the company that her husband built.

Rex couldn't understand how a woman who was brutally abused by her husband would want to protect anything that he owned. His mother was a different character.

She dressed her beloved husband smartly in a handsome suit and made sure that he had a proper burial. She begged and pleaded with her in laws to help pay for her husband's funeral. When they refused she walked away with her head held high.

Rex cried as he recalled his father's funeral. Dressed in their only white shirts and black slacks that were passed down from their older brother, they sat stoic in the front seat of the clapboard building. Their mother held them tight as she sat poised in the seat of the tiny white church.

Well wishers passed by and she acknowledged each one with a level of dignity and strength that he never seen before. His mother. The woman who he believed was as fragile as the one piece of china stashed in their cabinet.

This woman was completely different, she handled the funeral and burial arrangements on her own, while holding her remaining sons close to her chest.

She was a tiny woman only five feet tall with long brown curls and a bright white smile. Annie was his mother's name. Rex never loved another woman the way he loved his dear Annie. Her spirit remained with him, long after her death.

He smiled as her scent permeated the tiny office in the back of his Saloon. Annie was such a dear woman with the strength of a horse and the gentleness of a dove.

Annie would sit in the rocking chair, humming old tunes as she knitted or simply staring out the window. She was their entertainment on evenings before bed, weaving stories of old. She was the only person who could make them laugh hysterically from a story that she made up in her brilliant mind.

His mother never learned to read or write, but she urged

her boys to attend grade school. She made sure that they had all that they needed, including love.

After their father's death, she simply deteriorated in front of their eyes. It was if their brother Carl murdered both of his parents the day he killed their father. After his father's death, Carl's name was never spoken in the house again.

"Walk tall as the trees;
live strong as the
mountains, be gentle as
the spring winds, keep
the warmth of the
summer sun in your
heart, and the great spirit
will always be with you"

- Green Moss

Chapter 17

He sat for a moment, reflecting on his childhood. He could see his cousins playing in the water and running through their land. They had no idea that their lives would change so drastically. Dark Eagle prepared Redd Bird for life, but he never prepared him for death.

He rose and went about his business.

Redd was pleased when he noticed the rattlesnake hiding behind the bush. He was out hunting, searching for poison for his arrows. The heat Arizona desert was not a great place to locate poisonous frogs, he had to improvise. Staring at the bush he determined his approach.

Dark Eagle taught Redd and his cousins how to hunt for more than just food. He was unafraid, but respectful. His grandfather told him to respect the power of a snake.

100 times smaller than a human and unable to walk, the

snake was more deadly than anything he could come across. Many people who didn't respect the snake found themselves in dire pain as they awaited a painful death. Redd was not that type of person.

Although he didn't have a drop of fear in his heart, he had respect and it was with that respect that he approached the bush and gently reached down to grab the head of the creature. It thrashed and hissed, rattling its tail to provoke fear in Redd. Instead, he talked to it, informing the snake that he had no intention of hurting it. The snake, however didn't want to hear that as he tried his best to get away from Redd's strong grip.

With one hand he held the deadly head of the rattlesnake, with the other he grabbed the head. Using the tried and true methods of the great Dark Eagle he banged the head of the animal, stunning it for several minutes.

Using that precious time, Redd pulled the canister from his pocket and pressed the head against it. Suddenly, the teeth of the snake appeared. Redd pressed the teeth against the canister, humming a song taught to him by his grandfather.

As the deadly venom made its way from the mouth of the dangerous creature to the canister, Redd continued to steady himself. Once he was satisfied with the amount of venom in the canister, he tossed the creature several feet away from him.

Dark Eagle used to warn them that if they didn't put a foot worth of distance between them and the snake, it would seek revenge and it would win.

Dark Eagle taught them many things, Redd used them all making him the most lethal man in the west. When he returned to the camp his bride was preparing their meal. She looked up at him as he revealed the canister with a smile of success.

Returning his smile she walked up to him and placed a loving kiss on his lips, then she returned to the fire to continue nursing it. Redd wondered how he survived this long without a bride as sweet as his Catē.

She and his unborn child gave him the courage and the

motivation to work hard. He had two people to provide for now. That thought remained with him as he coated his arrows in the poison of the rattlesnake.

One arrow he allowed to soak inside the canister. This was the only arrow he would use to carry out his third mission. As his bride slept, he sat up on the thick blanket she hand sewed for the baby, he was in a state of peace, staring at the bright moon.

When the time was right, he stood and kissed his sleeping bride. She would remain inside the safety of the small, protected camp that he built for her. Their camp was located near a tucked away cave.

The gentleness of the wind pushed him as Midnight galloped along the dark road. They rode in the darkness for hours, until Redd reached his destination. His fourth victim rested peacefully in his bed as Redd watched him. He slept as if he didn't owe Caesar any money, as if there wasn't a bounty on his head.

It pained Redd to kill a sleeping man.

Instead, he walked towards the front of the house and began to bang on the old wooden door. When the man walked outside to investigate the noise, he stood face to face with Redd Bird.

Redd watched in amusement as a steam of water ran down the man's leg the moment he laid eyes on Redd Bird. His eyes went from that of an angry man to a wide eyed fearful expression, "P...p...please", the man begged. He was so afraid, he didn't try to hide the fact that he peed himself.

"I can pay you", he said trying to compose himself. "I have a wife", he began scratching at his head and mumbling. "I will give her to you", he said trying to sound as if he were offering him something. Redd simply stared at the man as he began pleading. He dropped to his knees, crying for mercy.

"You can take her", he said as tears ran down his face, mixing with the urine on the old porch. Redd Bird didn't say one word to the man. He began to fear that Redd Bird could understand what he was saying.

He ran inside his house to wake his wife as Redd stood watching the charade in amusement. When the man returned he was holding a hand full of gold. Redd gave the man a sad look. A man with a hand full of gold didn't make a different to Redd.

He would die regardless.

Redd turned and walked away as the man stood on the steps, hands outstretched holding the gold with tears running down his face.

Redd didn't like to play games, but the fact that this man had money and decided not to pay his debts irked him. Especially the fact that he would rather part with his wife before parting with his money.

What kind of lily livered man would offer his wife as a form of payment, to save his own life. The thought made Redd Bird sick to his stomach. He usually felt at least some pang of sympathy for his victims. They usually were hard working poor folks, simply trying to survive.

This man was not deserving of his sympathy.

As he walked away he pulled the bow up on his shoulder. He expertly released the venom-soaked arrow directly into the man's left lung without ever facing his target.

Chapter 18

Silo counted her bounty as she applauded herself,
impressed by her deeds. She only needed several more
boosts to ensure that she would never have to return
home or marry to be taken care of.

Her long braids were chopped off at the neck and she
was dressed in the pants and clothing of the poor
gentleman who drove the stagecoach. She was growing
quite smart about her surroundings. Silo knew that only
men received respect under the heat of the Arizona
desert.

Since she felt that she too was deserving of more than
just respect, she made a plan to do what she needed to
do. Silo loved a different type of emotion – she wanted
to be feared. Her wants lead her to make drastic changes
to her once lovely appearance. The man who attacked
her could have easily over powered her if she didn't have
the physical and mental prowess that she possessed.

She was grateful for the attack. It helped her become

who she really was, a force to be reckoned with.

Creeping behind the two men walking outside of the dimly lit Saloon. She didn't understand a lot of English, but she taught herself a few key words, by reading newspapers. She found that many folk discarded their previously read newspapers throughout the land without a care.

She knew that in her homeland they would never have been so careless as to discard their trash in the same place where they slept, farmed and lived. It disgusted her, but there were many things about these foreign pale faced people that unnerved her.

She tried her best to steer clear of them; or at least until it was time to rob them. In her mind that was their only significance to ensure her survival.

Chopping off her hair and dressing in male attire would also help her conceal her identity when the law came looking. She covered her short hair with the dusty hat of her latest victim.

Moving only in the darkness, she had become a legend in the desert in a short span of time. Yet no one knew of her true identity and she wanted to keep it that way.

When she poked the man standing closest to her with the gun, they both turned quickly with their hands on their pistols in the holster. They both turned bright red as they noticed that their pistols were missing.

Another lethal gift of Silo's. She was a stealth and silent as a snake trying to attack their prey.

The looks on their faces made her guffaw as she showed them their guns. "How", one man began to question how she got ahold of their guns without their knowledge. As she held their guns against them, the men began to reach in their pockets.

"Hands up", she commanded in broken English. The men understood exactly what she wanted. She watched as one man reached in both pockets, emptying them before her. While the other man boldly turned to run. She didn't bend to pick up the money, nor did she move to chase the man who bolted. Instead she raised the pistol and shot the man in the head with his own pistol. Never flinching, she turned to face the now terrified man.

"Please don't kill me", he began to beg and plead for his life, using words that she couldn't understand, but she understood fear. It was written all over his face.

Silo motioned for the man to leave, but he remained begging for his life. She figured that he didn't want to be shot in the head as his friend who was lying three feet away from them. She could smell his fear. It didn't faze her, though. She used to feel sorry for her victims, but after her fourth robbery she finally got used to the feeling.

In fact, she enjoyed the entire thing. The preparation the planning and the execution, she enjoyed it all. There was something about power and fear that felt like a high to her. After the taste of this type of power she vowed to never return to the days of old.

She motioned with the pistol for him to leave, but he

stood there for a moment, watching Silo gather the gold coins, placing them in her pocket. When he turned his attention to her again, she was gone.

The man stood there with his hands still in the air; an air thick with fear and death.

Chapter 19

Beth Anne wiped the bar down and watched as the waitresses left for the night. "Evenin'", she heard the last patron call out to her as he walked out the bar. She let out an exhausted sigh. "Evenin' Bud", she said to one of her most annoying customers as he stumbled out the door.

As soon as he made it out the door, she heard him collapse in a dusty heap out front. The large cloud of dust sent dirt all through the air.

She didn't mind him when he was placing money in her hand, but after he had a few drinks, he was like the others in the bar. Sloppy, loud and rowdy. After working at the bar for nearly five years, the slightest things they did annoyed her.

She was worried about her boss. He spent the entire day and evening locked inside his office. The last time she saw him this way he was facing legal troubles with Sherriff Kyle, their small town's only Sherriff.

Beth Anne talked to the Sherriff and was able to help Rex out of his legal troubles. Hell, she did more than talk to him. That was the main reason why Rex made her the head waitress of the Saloon. After lying under that sweaty fat bastard for one night, she told him he owed her as much.

The night sky was a dark blanket with several stars sprinkled about. Satisfied with the evening's revenue, Rex walked home feeling gleeful. He knew that he had to do something to secure the other half of his debt, and soon.

He thought about collecting on all of his owed tabs, even going as far as posting signs on the doors and bar wall informing patrons that if they had a debt they needed to pay it. Rex didn't expect many people to pay him, but to his surprise, he was approached by three men wanting to pay their bills. Though their combined $350 didn't put a dent in his debt, he was grateful for them.

After thinking about it for several hours, Rex made his mind up.

He waited in his bar until nightfall because what he planned to do he needed to do under the cloak of darkness. Rex couldn't bare to imagine how terrible things would have been for him and his family if he were caught doing what he needed to do.

Chapter 20

The sun rose over the canyon lighting a fire in the blue sky. He was already awake and staring out at the vast canyon below. Being in the canyon was one of the signs that there was something bigger than them out there. There was something about watching the sunrise.

It seemed as if the earth was still and asleep, wiping the sleep and grogginess from the corner of its eye. It was early in the morning, but the haze from the sun was already visible. He could tell the day would be quite hot, but that wasn't something that bothered him.

He made changes since he met his bride. He laughed as he recalled a conversation about change with his grandfather. "A river can not change its path", he once told him about change. He wondered if he was doing his grandfather justice, living the way he did.

He traveled under the darkness of early morning, never during the middle day. It was the best way to ensure that his bride was protected. It took much restraint to leave her alone, but he knew that he had work to do.

He thought about the most recent job. How much the man begged and pleaded for his life, only to offer his wife, his main reason for living as a lifesaver. It angered him. He was incredulous. His wife was more precious than anything to him.

His bride slept in the camp, as peaceful as a dove. He loved how peaceful she slept as if there were not a bounty on his head and two people left on his hit list. She didn't know and would never know how dangerous their situation truly was.

He took the jobs because he needed to put distance between him and his previous employers henchmen. He wasn't sure of it, but he knew that someone was out there, ready to avenge the murder of their boss.

He was a smart man, not because of his education but due to his wit. His ear rested solely to the ground, making him very aware.

Redd could see his target shuffling around his small general store. Harlen King was a man without a soul. He walked around the store, aimlessly placing price tags on his short supply of items. It was early in the morning and Harlen had a lot of work to do.

He stopped to gawk out the window for a moment. His assistant, Bettie was due in at any time. He loved Bettie, she was the real reason why he kept the store open after 20 years. He wanted to close the store and retire, but there was no way he could do that.

His debts were too high.

He knew his loan shark would be sending someone out to get him soon. That's why he devised a plan. He already had his bags packed. His wife was home preparing their things. She knew that they needed to move, quickly, but didn't know the reason.

Harlen felt like he owed her that much. At this point, peace of mind was all he could give her.

The bell to the front door rang, just as Harlen was contemplating his thoughts. He knew it was Bettie and looked in the tiny mirror above his filing cabinets, in his tiny office.

He smoothed his hair and chewed on a piece of mint that his wife kept for him, for luck she claimed.

"Bettie, we need to talk", he said walking outside to face his real true love. When he walked inside the store, he couldn't find Bettie. "Bettie", he called out, thinking she was in the back, already preparing supper to serve to weary cow folk.

When his eyes focused on the red man staring him down from the front door. "C..can I", he couldn't get the words out before the bullet hit his head, dropping him to the ground. After filling his sack with delectable groceries, the man was gone in a flash.

Ten minutes later, Bettie arrive to a bloody scene. She screamed when she saw her boss and lover gunned down in the aisle. "Who could have done such a thing", she demanded as she screamed in the face of the poor

Sherriff, Kyle. The man simply walked around the bloody scene and shook his head, sadly. "I don't know Bettie, but don't worry. We will capture him", he responded, comforting the sad, large chested woman, as she cried on his chest.

He knew in his heart that Harlen was gunned down by a professional. It was only one bullet to the head and no evidence was left behind. "Redd Bird", he mumbled under his breath, shaking his head.

Chapter 21

Darkness fell as quickly as she moved. Silo stretched and yawned, loudly. She frightened her horse who was resting nearby. "It's time", she whispered both to herself and her horse. She had enough items in her bag to last her for days and enough money to last for years, but she wanted more.

Money, security and the ease of it all were haunting her.

She became so skilled at what she did, it was a wonderful thing. She could hear her great-grandmother's voice in her ear, "The more you are thankful the more you attract things to be more thankful for". She nodded her head in agreement.

Her great-grandmother was a wise woman.

She sat there for a while, contemplating what her great grandmother revealed to her. As she dressed in the worn pants and shirt complete with boots that were five sizes bigger than her feet, Silo looked in the tin mirror and smiled at her reflection. Her hair was still cropped quite short. Under the security of darkness, no one would see that she was a woman.

As she and her horse eased down the canyon and headed towards the dimly lit town, she devised her plan. Sneaking slowly behind the coral of horses, Silo decided that she would take the next man who came out of the Saloon. The horses and their stench were almost too much for her stomach to take, but she reminded herself what was at hand.

She could make herself a rich woman, if she just completed a few more jobs. That's what she considered what she was doing, a job. Silo reasoned that she was only taking a small amount of money from the men, they had enough to survive off.

She wasn't there long before her next target began stumbling out of the Saloon. He was singing loudly and walking in a zig zag motion. Silo stifled a laugh. Before the man reached his horse, she dodged out in front of him with the rifle aimed at his face.

The drunkard gave her a silly smile and threw his hands up in the air. She motioned for him to empty his pockets, but instead the man pulled out a pistol. Silo shot the man with her rifle before he had a chance to place his finger on the trigger.

The loud blast drew everyone out of the Saloon. Silo slinked to her horse and climbed on his back as they left the property, undetected.

Little did she knew, someone was watching her every move, waiting for the opportunity to strike.

"Make me always ready to come to you with clean hands and straight eyes so that when my life fades as the fading sunset. My spirit can come to you without shame"

- Dark Eagle

Chapter 22

Redd Bird and Catē arrived into town in a ball of dust. He was in a hurry. They traveled a great distance and along the way he was able to take out the last name on the list. He was grateful and ready to get to his homeland. They were less than a day away from reaching it.

When he walked to the door of Caesar's home he had a sinking feeling in his stomach. Instinctively, he checked his side holsters for his two .45 pistols. Although he enjoyed using the bow and arrow for his art, he still kept guns on both side.

Guns were lethal and quick but required less skill. He enjoyed the process of locating poison, soaking and sharpening his arrows; the sound of the arrow as it flew from the force of the bow. That was what Redd Bird liked to do.

As usual he told Catē to remain on the back of the horse and he knocked on the door again. He tried the knob and saw that it was locked. He called out to the man,

"Caesar, you in there", but there was only silence in return.

Frustrated, he hopped off the porch and walked around to the back of the house. He noticed that the back door was wide open. Redd Bird walked through the house with his .45 in his right hand, ready to shoot.

When he walked through the door, he noticed Caesar lying on the floor in a thick puddle of his own blood. Redd Bird saw the slit across the man's throat from one end to the other. He couldn't believe it, someone took the man out, long before he had the chance.

He searched through the man's items looking for his money. Whomever killed the man wiped him out. Redd Bird was so angry he could've spit. He walked out the house empty handed and returned to his bride.

To his horror, Catē was lying on the ground writhing in pain. He ran to her in a panic. This was not happening. He tried to ask her what was wrong when he looked at the bottom of her dress, which was covered in blood. She was having trouble with the baby.

He pulled out blankets and gave her cold water. He didn't know what to do beyond that. She was crying out in pain and he was powerless to do anything. He placed a pillow under her legs trying to make her as comfortable as possible.

They were there for hours. Redd Bird kept his pistol at his side to ensure that they remained safe, while his wife delivered their child.

The look of agony on her face gave Redd pause. He was terrified of what could happen to his wife and child without their doctor.

Catē tried her best to stand as he helped her to a standing position. Redd could tell by the agony on her face that she was in trouble. He couldn't think of a doctor anywhere nearby. His heart filled with dread. He knew what she was trying to do. She was trying to deliver the baby on her own, knowing that standing might be the easiest way to deliver it.

He suddenly heard what he thought was a nanny goat crying. Redd reached out and grabbed his baby. In his heart, seeing his wife in that manner, he thought they both were doomed. Holding his son, he felt an overwhelming emotion like never before.

He reached down and showed the baby to his wife. That was when he noticed that her eyes were closed.

His bride died on the same ground where his dreams were buried.

That day Redd Bird lost a great piece of him.

Chapter 23

The bugs were making noises as if they were announcing his arrival. The large house sat on a hill thick with trees and brush. Snakes, scorpions and the like loved to crawl in areas like this waiting on their prey. Rex thought about the irony of that. He too was waiting on his prey.

He watched through the windows, the house was completely dark. This was great because the last thing Rex needed was to be detected. He tiptoed towards the front window and noticed that it was open.

He smiled to himself. This thing just might work out.

As he climbed through the window, he removed his shoes. He had been in the house before and knew that the floors were wood which echoed loudly against his boots. Rex walked towards the back of the house where the old man's office resided.

He knew that the old man was fast asleep upstairs. He

could hear the snoring from his place at the foot of the stairs. Rex arrived at the office and used his lighter to illuminate the small room. His father won the expensive trinket at a card game years ago. Rex was given everything that his father had.

He wiped the tear away from his cheek. He didn't realize that he was crying until another tear hit the desk. "Get it together Rex", he commanded himself softly. He cried every time he thought of his father. He wasn't a good man, but Rex still loved him dearly.

He pulled the drawer on the right side of the desk open and to his surprise it was filled with gold coins. He mentally thanked Bettie Anne for her help. She went home with the old man two days prior. He needed to know if Leven was really as wealthy as he claimed to be.

Rex had to promise Bettie Anne a raise for doing his dirty work. She didn't know what his plans were, but something told him that Bettie Anne knew exactly what he was planning to do. She gave him the information without a question. That told him that she already made the answer up in her own mind.

As he tossed the coins in his potato sack he let out a relieved sigh. He would finally be able to pay his bills and maybe buy his wife and Beth Anne something nice. Rex was getting excited, planning what he would do with the money. He could give Lance every dollar he owed with interest.

Rex was considering redoing the Saloon. The place looked exactly as it did when his father owned it. The only thing he changed was adding a small stage for the waitresses to dance for the customers. It was time for a facelift.

Everything would be different for Rex. He now had money. Rex was so excited. He closed the drawer and turned to leave the dark room.

That was when he heard the familiar click of a .45 pistol.

Epilogue

Following closely behind the murderer, Earl and his horse were on the trail. He had a plan and plenty of gun power to carry out the plan. This man was skilled, he took down men with no regard, but Earl was also skilled. Quick witted and a quick draw, Earl knew that he would be able to avenge his father's murder.

He covered his body in a black drape, hoping to hide himself under the darkness. Earl knew everything about this man who took his father's life and money. He knew that the man only traveled in darkness. He studied his moves as he watched him take down several targets.

Earl was ready for battle and if he died in battle at least he died with dignity.

He recalled the Sherriff staring absently as he told him about his father's murder. He acted like his hands were tied. Earl knew that look, it was fear. How could the Sherriff fear someone? It bothered Earl that the men in the town had no tenacity. They didn't want to get involved in anything that was dangerous. Earl didn't care. He knew that the killer was skilled, but it didn't matter. Earl was skilled in hand to hand fighting. With fire red hair, freckles and the ability to turn the color of his hair when he was angry, he had no choice.

Teased relentlessly in grade school, Earl had developed a chip on his shoulder.

He was angry with his father. He told the old man not to hire red men. He knew that they were nothing but trouble, but his father claimed that he trusted the man who eventually took his life. "See there Pop", he said to the sky. "You didn't believe in me, but I will show you", he declared as he and his target slowed down.

Earl watched as his target stopped at their camp and tied the horse to the post.

He knew exactly what he would do. Climbing off his horse, he grabbed his gun and laid on his stomach watching the red faced man.

The element of surprise was the best way to handle this lethal man. He watched as the man spread his blanket and laid down for sleep. Earl wanted to run to the man and demand a reason for killing his father. Instead, he waited patiently as the red faced man slept.

An hour later, Earl decided to strike. His gun drawn and his boots off, he tiptoed to the red faced man's camp. The darkness was thick enough to cover them both. His target couldn't see him and suddenly he could no longer find his target.

Before he had a chance to search, he could hear the pistol clicking behind him. His heart began to gallop like his horse. The sound startled Earl. Then the fear began to settle into his heart. This man was good at what he did.

He turned to face the man who killed his father. "Why", he demanded as he stomped his foot on the ground. "Why kill my daddy", he wanted a reason from the angry man. The man threw the pistol to the ground as Earl let out a sigh.

Maybe he wouldn't kill Earl.

Maybe he realized the error in his ways, for killing his father.

Earl began walking away from the man, when suddenly a shotgun was produced. He could tell that the man didn't understand what he was saying. Earl began to weep as he stared down the barrel of a shotgun. He held the pistol tight in his hands, ready to shoot.

Silo stared at the man sadly, before she leveled the shotgun and fired. The bloody body collapsed to the ground in front of Silo. She was shaken. How did this man find her camp?

A pain in her side caused her to fall down next to the man. She touched her side and realized that it was wet. As the excruciating pain ripped through her entire body, she grabbed at her side and saw the blood covering her hand.

Silo had been shot.

Staring at the dark sky, she called out to her ancestors, "Make me always ready to come to you with clean hands and straight eyes so that when my life fades as the fading sunset. My spirit can come to you without shame", she declared.

She died there with the man who stalked her for days, never knowing that she was not the person who killed his father.

Silo died never understanding why the man was after her in the first place.

"The tragedy of life is not death but what we let die within while we live"

- Dark Eagle

In the Clouds

CREEK

To begin anew, one must be willing to release the old.

- Dark Eagle

Prologue

A cloud of dust trailed behind him as he rode into town on the shiny brown horse. Studying the land around him he seemed pleased to finally be in the dusty town. He clutched the map tightly in his hands and compared the town name with that of the map, Town Springs.

It was a small spot on the map, but based on what he saw, the place was heavily populated, which meant only one thing.

Money!

For as long as he could recall, folks referred to The West like it was akin to a gold mine, literally. Fathers, husbands and sons packed up their belongings and hauled it out of town, heading to the West for prospecting.

Lemieux's own brother hit it big out in Kansas in the gold mines. Although he wanted a piece of the pie, Lemieux knew that he was expected to make his own way.

Lemieux watched his brother intently and hung on every word his parents said about him. He too wanted to head out West once he was old enough. His brother, Sam was nearly ten years older and had a much bigger advantage as the oldest son.

When it was time for Lemieux to set out on his own, the gold mines had dried up. Folks were losing their entire fortune trying to make it big in a market that could no longer support them.

He watched as town residents walked about the small wooden walkways crisscrossing the town. They strutted about aimlessly. He watched men and women stumble around the entryway to the grocery store, Saloon and stables, all of them blissfully unaware.

They all seemed to be in a contented stupor, walking around with serene smiles on their faces.

Chuckling to himself, he placed the map back inside his saddle as images rushed through his head. These people had no idea what was about to happen to their tiny town.

They would never be the same.

Lemieux looked around the dusty town and hocked a wad of spit on the ground. He hated traveling out West, but the stories he heard about the riches buried in the dust bowl town, he had to make his way out there.

He worked tirelessly for three days straight surveying the town, making sure that his efforts would not be in vain.

He was on a mission.

Get in and get out was his motto. The words replayed in his head constantly, "$2,000 or she dies," his tormentor teased knowing that there wasn't a snowball's chance in hell that Lemieux would ever come up with the money.

The fact that his wife was being held captive motivated

Lemieux to do the implausible; he was going to go down in history as a famous man, although no one knew his name.

They would one day.

He had to make as much money as possible in the shortest time, or else his family would be several members short.

Chapter 1

"Can I help you?" he asked before poking his head out from under the counter. "Naw", said the grungy looking man traipsing through the store. He seemed out of place in the prim and proper town, but Ray was not a man to judge others by their looks. He prided himself on being a Christian man, which prevented him from judging.

He absently patted the Bible sitting on the counter near him. He spent a great deal of time reading the Bible, not only was it a source of comfort for the old man, it was the only book he knew how to read.

Truthfully, he couldn't read it, but he memorized scriptures that he enjoyed reading to impress the poor folks who knew nothing about being a Christian. His relatives prided themselves on their mission to convert the Indian from their "savage" ways and help them accept Christ in their lives.

It was not an easy task, but one that the Tourtens prided themselves on, nonetheless.

When the straggly looking man made his way to the front of the store, Ray nearly jumped from fright. His memory wasn't long at all and he had completely forgotten about the man until he noticed a familiar silver glint in the man's left hand.

A damn shotgun!

The shotgun was aimed at the terrified man as he scrambled trying his best to gather the money from the rickety register as quickly as possible. "Hurry, Pops", the man wielding the gun screamed, motioning with the gun towards the cash register.

"I'm...trying", the man responded as the sweat dripped from his forehead to the tip of his nose and his heart pounded in his chest.

Ray had been working at King's General for nearly three decades. In all of his years, he never experienced anything like what he was going through at the moment. He glared at the angry, slim man standing in front of him holding the gun and wondered where his life went wrong.

Handing the bag of money to the man, he kicked himself for not bringing his gun with him to work. He carried it with him for years after the first stagecoach robbery in the dusty town, refusing to ever be a victim.

"Now look at me," he said to himself as the dirty vermin snatched the bag of money and looked Ray square in the eyes. "I gave you what you asked for," he pleaded with the criminal. "Let me live", he begged as the man spit on the floor and snatched the hat off his head, revealing his identity.

"I'm sorry", he offered aiming the shotgun at Ray's chest and pulling the trigger. He couldn't explain the way he felt, but he really was sorry for doing what he had to do. Sorry that he had to kill and more remorseful that it was only the beginning.

Lemieux was on a journey, thanks to his tormentor, he would forever be changed.

True peace comes when you can look at another's behavior toward you as a symptom of their relationship with themselves rather than an indication of your character.

- Dark Eagle

Chapter 2

They sat at the bank of the flowing river admiring the beauty of the prairie. He was proud to be on the land that his ancestors cultivated and labored over to make their own. After days of riding and camping, he finally made it back home. It was a bittersweet moment, without his Catē.

He carried his wife back with him to bury her on their sacred grounds. Although it was a long difficult ride, he rejoiced when he returned to his home. For once, he felt at peace.

Watching his son play in the water he felt satisfied with his decision to return to their lands, at least for a while. The women in the village sprung into action the moment they heard about Catē's death.

Redd Bird chuckled as he recalled their keen interest in him and his young handsome son. He knew that soon he would have to take a wife, and so did they. Rising Sun needed a mother; he needed someone to care for him. Redd loved his son, but he wasn't the type to rear a child on his own.

The women in their village were well aware of that. The Creek women were a beautiful, strong and sturdy type of woman. He knew that no matter who he chose, she wouldn't compete with his deceased bride, but he also knew that any of the women in their town would take excellent care of his son.

Blue Moon was a gorgeous woman, nearly a decade younger than Redd Bird, but everywhere he turned she was right there, willing to help.

She secured a nursemaid for his son and ensured that he was well-fed and kept. That meant a great deal to Redd. Blue Moon cared more about his son than he could've ever imagined.

When he thanked her for taking care of his son, she responded sweetly, "This is all I know how to do. Care". It was something about her posture and position that made Redd look at her more than once in a loving manner.

He admired her for doing what she did for him. There was only a few areas that Redd Bird felt entirely secure and none of them included caring for a baby.

He was good at only a few things, murder was one of them; parenting was not. Rising Sun splashed around in the water, squealing with glee as Redd sharpened the spear in his hand, staring intently at the water below.

The moment the fish made a turn in front of the patient man, he struck capturing the large fish on the sharp end of the spear. Redd turned to look at his son and smiled at the look of awe on the boy's face. "Soon, my son", he urged as visions of him teaching Rising Sun how to fish and hunt on the same land where he was taught.

Redd Bird still couldn't believe it after six months, he was a father. Rising Sun needed someone to be his guide, his leader and teacher. He would be to Rising Sun what Dark Eagle was to him.

From the moment he lost his precious Catē, he vowed

that he would do his best for their son. He recalled the eagles soaring above them, circling as his wife took her last breath.

He knew in his heart that his grandfather was telling him that he would take care of them. The four eagles followed them from that dusty road to their home. Redd couldn't help but look above as he listened to his son giggle at the fish splashing around him.

The eagles were still there, waiting. They too heard the voice of his grandfather urging Redd Bird to continue on his journey. Redd was disappointed by the request of Dark Eagle. He couldn't bear to do what his grandfather wanted him to do, but something told him that it was for the very best.

The sun left footprints on the sky as darkness began to fall. Redd had been stalling long enough. "Yes, grandfather," he replied to the howling wind. As his son played in the water he stared at the sky, ending his conversation with his grandfather, Dark Eagle.

It was settled.

Gazing out at the prairie below his modest home, Trig sat his teacup on the table and closed his eyes. The wind had suddenly picked up, causing tiny bits of dust to lift from the ground, irritating his eyes. "I hate this place," he declared to no one in particular.

He could have stood on the top of his house and yelled to the wind, but no one would hear him. Having acquired the large farm four years ago, Trig enjoyed the seclusion of his own 144-acre property. The estate was littered with structures to house his possessions and protect his livelihood.

Trig was not originally from the West. After being discharged from the Army he hightailed it out of town. Having moved out there with his brother and cousin a decade prior in search of riches, Trig left his Alabama home without looking back.

His pockets were sagging with the money from his inheritance. His father died from a horrible case of Yellow Fever, leaving Trig and his younger brother

Stetson to fed for themselves.

His brother conceded that he would run the family farm to carry on the legacy of their father and grandfather. Trig on the other hand had no time to tend to frivolous things such as legacies, to him legacies didn't make him money and that was the only thing on Trig's mind, money.

So, after packing his belongings and bidding his brother adieu, Trig was bolting headfirst into his future. Sadly, the land dried up the same year his father died. The drought lasted the entire season, threatening starvation across the town.

Trig and Stetson managed to survive off tiny rations and their stock piling from the years before. In an effort to escape the empty feeling in his stomach, Trig hoisted himself on the back of his horse and hightailed it out of the depressing town.

There was nothing more for him in his hometown. After hearing about the luck his friends were having out West, he decided to hop on the train.

It was time to put the inheritance to good use.

And here he was, standing at the base of his property surveying all that he had amassed. He was really proud of himself and knew that his father and brother would be proud as well.

The thought made him smile broadly as he brought the teacup to his lips for a sip of the sweet hot liquid.

Suddenly, he noticed the dust standing up at the far end of the road, signaling a visitor. Squinting his eyes for a better view, he watched as the rider made their way to the front of the driveway.

Emil climbed off the horse and secured it to the post before dusting off his shoes and hat with his hand. Trig rolled his eyes at the sight of the overly proper man.

Although he trusted Emil a great deal, his mannerisms were maddening. He listened as Emil pounded on the front door of his home and then stood back to admire his reflection in the window.

"Emil, howdy," he called out waving to his friend. "Howdy, partna," Emil said somberly shaking the man's hand. "What's the problem," Trig asked instantly noting Emil's body language.

"We gotta problem, boss," Emil replied removing his hat.

INCLINE YOUR EARS TO THE
WIND. HEAR THE WISDOM OF
YOUR ANCESTORS.

- CATĒ

Chapter 4

The wind blew mightily as he un-fastened the tent and stepped outside to feel the rush of air on his skin. "Yes, grandfather," he called out with his arms spread open wide.

He could feel the strength of Dark Eagle fusing with his own weary spirit. It gave him hope. Falling to his knees, he meditated as his grandfather's spirit connected with his own. An hour later, he stood with new purpose. His bride was gone, but he had a responsibility. He had someone that needed him.

For that reason, he began packing and preparing his things for his next trip. He didn't know where he was being led, but the moment he saw the wind lift the small specks of sand from the ground and stir them in a circle, he knew that his grandfather would serve as his guide. That made him comfortable and ready for the new journey.

He stared at his young son, resting peacefully in his

basket without a care in the world. It truly broke his heart to do what he had to do next.

Under the cloak of darkness, Redd Bird walked towards Blue Moon's dwelling. He felt terrible about entering the home of an unmarried woman but his grandfather's voice urged him to do so.

He stopped several feet in front of the house and paced for a moment, unsure of what to say. Suddenly a strong gush of wind pushed Redd, urging him to the door.

Blue Moon rubbed her lovely almond eyes and gave Redd a sleepy grin. She looked around as if she were confused. "Where is Rising Sun", she inquired. "At home sleeping. I'm sorry to disturb you, but I really need your help", he pleaded as she wrapped her long robe around her shapely body and nodded for him to continue speaking.

"I have been sent on another journey and I..." Redd's voice trailed off as he tried to conjure up a way to ask for her help. She didn't give him a chance to respond. Instead, she held her hand up high and told him, "it would be my pleasure to look after Rising Sun", she said smiling brightly.

A sudden gust of wind lifted her hair, teasing his nostrils with the sensuous scent of Sandalwood and Berries. His grandfather's voice spoke loudly in his ear. Redd nearly jumped out of his skin at the sound of his voice. He wanted to tell his grandfather, "no". There was no way he would go through with Dark Eagle's plan.

Shaking his head, he imagined that his grandfather had lost some of his mind in his departure from this life. "I don't know when I will return", he said quickly trying his best not to hear the words he was speaking. Here he was, abandoning his only child. It didn't sit right with him.

He watched the expression on Blue Moon's face change and wondered what it was all about. When she bowed her head and whispered, "yes" he already knew what was transpiring.

"I will journey with you", Blue Moon responded with a satisfied smile. Redd Bird didn't know what to say. He simply returned her smile and turned on his heels. "Gather your things. We leave at sunrise", he responded as she bowed and closed the door. As he walked back to the home he shared with Rising Sun, Redd Bird couldn't help but stare at the sky and shake his head.

Grandfather always had the last word.

DISRESPECT IS AN ILLNESS.
ONCE DISRESPECT IS
TOLERATED IT BEGINS TO
PROLIFERATE LIKE AN INSIPID
DISEASE.

- THE GENERAL

Chapter 5

"Ray, Murdered?" he repeated as Emil continued explaining the situation going on in the next town. Trig swallowed his anger and tried his best to keep his composure. Emotion was something that he didn't show often. It was a weakness that the wealthy man couldn't afford.

Unlike his neighbors, who were legitimate bankers and store owners he had a different type of reputation to protect. The consequences of bad business situations were far more severe and often deadly.

He took a swig of the whiskey and let out a sigh reaching for his smokes in his shirt pocket Trig stewed over the information he had just received from his dear friend and colleague. He really wanted to do some damage because this information was not what he expected to get.

One of his stores, a front for his moonshine business was hit and his best friend Ray was murdered. He tried his best to keep his emotions together, but he felt the warm tear as it trickled down his worn face. He couldn't believe that this was happening to him. "Who would dare steal from me?" he demanded slamming his fist on the table sending his whiskey bottle into a shaking frenzy for a several seconds.

His proverbial question tainted the air like the foul smell of a pigs pen.

Trig was a vicious man, known in Santa Fe as, "The General", he had enough blood on his hands to be a war criminal in most countries. The name came from his brief stint in the United States Army. Although he was an excellent soldier his tenure in the Corps wasn't very long.

Trig was never one to take orders from anyone, which was not the type of personality for a situation such as the Army, but Trig didn't realize his mistake until his first day. The moment he stepped off the bus, he was yelled at and shoved to the ground by his Superior, Lt. Conrad.

Trig retaliated with a swift punch to his superiors jaw. The broken jaw situation didn't go over well with the higher ups. It especially didn't help that Emil wasn't remorseful in the least. He wanted to get his superior something terrible and that's just what he did.

It wasn't until his graduation from boot camp that he decided to enact his revenge. Trig was dangerous in that way. He held grudges and plotted like it was a full time job. Once he was hurt or betrayed he simply nodded and smiled all the while plotting his revenge.

He was a patient man, one who could wait weeks, months even years to strike, and his strike was a deadly one.

Lt. Conrad was standing in front of the mirror in his bedroom at the barracks, admiring his reflection. He was officiating the graduation ceremony and had to look his sharpest.

The 62 year old man was also preparing to retire from his position. Appraising his reflection in the mirror, he sat his hat on top of his thinning white hair and straightened it.

He was looking forward to retirement. Reaching for the picture on the dresser of he and Mrs. Conrad made him smile. He dedicated his entire life to the Army and his service to the country, at the expense of his marriage and family. He had five sons and three daughters who were all adults and didn't know him at all. Before he could catch it, tears began to ebb and flow down his face.

Overcome by sorrow, he didn't hear the door open behind him nor did he feel the first strike of the baseball bat. 25 stiches, a broken rib and fractured arm and a dishonorable discharge later, Trig bid his adieu to the Uncle Sam.

A year later he found himself sleeping on his brothers sofa in their two bedroom trailer and realized that this was not the life he wanted for himself. That was when he met Ray. He and Ray came up with their moonshining plan and from there they began investing in businesses and skimming off the top.

Within five years, Trig earned enough money to purchase his grand ranch. His shrewd business skills earned him a great deal of money while his ruthless attitude won him respect.

Respect was the name of the game. A single act of disrespect could render someone injured, broke or dead. Trig was not one to allow disrespect to go on. Disrespect was like an illness. Once disrespect is tolerated it begins to proliferate like an insipid disease.

Someone had committed the ultimate disrespect and they had to pay.

Chapter 6

They rode in complete silence. Both of them lost in their own thoughts. Redd Bird knew better than to question his elders and ancestors, but he couldn't understand the purpose for taking his young son on the road with him.

Who knew what he would face? Not only did he have his most precious gift to protect, he also had a beautiful young woman who needed his security.

He glanced at the lovely face of Blue Moon. She truly was a rarity. The sun shone on her face as she gently and calmly nursed his son. "Thank you", he said watching her with an appreciative smile.

He wondered how she was able to nurse his child when she had no children, but he couldn't bring himself to ask her. He reasoned with himself that she would tell him when she was ready.

Add that to the fact that the last thing he wanted to do right now was tend to an emotional woman. Since she and Rising Sun were content so was he.

Almost on cue, she turned to face him. "I can take care of you two", she offered with pleading eyes. Redd knew exactly what she was indicating, but he couldn't take her up on her offer. "I will make you happy", she begged as Redd held his hand up, halting her speech.

Redd had to clear his mind constantly. Although, he tried to ignore the nagging feeling, he hated the fact that this woman was with him and not his Catē. It burdened his heart that she would be snatched from his life at the most important time of their lives.

It hurt him deeply, but he had to push the pain aside and care for his son. That would be his homage to his Catē. He didn't want the girl to feel rejected, but there was no room in his heart for her. He tried to find the words to tell her so. Instead, he stood and walked away from the camp site, under the darkness the eagle traveled with him.

Both deep in thought.

Chapter 7

Smoke billowed from the roof of the house indicating that there were people inside the dwelling, but there was no movement anywhere near the outside of the house making him feel safe but not necessarily secure.

It all seemed way to perfect for Lemieux.

Pulling out his binoculars he glared directly in the windows of the log home. Watching the folks move around inside, he knew that she was in there.

She had to be.

He missed his wife dearly, but he also knew that she would be as mad as a hornet about the trouble he caused for their family. That recollection slowed his rescue efforts, a bit.

This was all his fault.

Gambling debts were the reason why he was on the run. It would take him a lifetime to save the kind of money his tormentor requested. It all happened so fast. He woke up one morning to an empty house.

His wife was gone and in her place was a note. The note read: "Pay or else".

He knew what that meant.

Lemieux hadn't worked in weeks due to the recent drought. Many of the cattle that he worked herding were dying out because of lack of food and water. This was truly a trying time for Lemieux. He drowned his sorrows in whiskey, until that fateful night.

He was sitting at the Broken Spittoon, a small hole in the wall Saloon, drowning his demons when a young lad came up to him and asked him to play a game of poker with the fellas.

He swallowed his pride, picked up his gun and went on a mission. He didn't have time to reminisce. If he didn't act soon he was going to be in a really bad position. He couldn't let the blood of his wife be on his hands.

"Better it be someone else's blood", he thought as he cocked the gun and fired in the air. "Alright hands up!", he screamed.

"The grave is the most valuable of places...a resting abode for priceless dreams"

- Catē

Chapter 8

Redd cradled his son in his arms as he made his bed more comfortable. He tried his best not to wake Blue Moon. It wasn't waking her that bothered him, it was the conversation that was sure to ensue.

He only needed to look down at his content boy and realize that Blue was a treasure. The boy was already surrounded by thick brightly colored blankets, all baring some relation to the color blue. Blue Moon hand wove the heavy blankets and each one served a purpose for the little one. She was a treasure, just not his.

He wondered what Catē would have said if she were there with them. Redd could feel her presence, it was as if his whole body was bathed in warmth. He cradled Rising Sun to his body as if he were hugging his family close to him.

Redd couldn't forgive himself. After all of the things he was able to do, all of the assignments he had been on. He couldn't keep his wife safe. He knew better than to question.

What was done had to be done and he had to find a way to be alright with it. Peace without full understanding was the way his people lived their lives. They never questioned their circumstances, they were taught to continue forward with their lives and allow their journey to play out however it was planned. This also protected them from a great deal of health troubles.

Redd chuckled at the way the boy snuggled in his blankets, seeming completely content with the world. Redd wished in his heart that he could keep the world that way for his son, but he knew better.

War had been ravishing the settlements of Sioux, Piscataway and some Creek tribes. Although, war existed for as long as his ancestors roamed the lands, this was a different type of war.

One initiated by outsiders. They pinned the tribes against each other, in hopes that they would wipe each other out.

Redd knew how resilient his people were. They withstood some of the most difficult times ever, taught those who invaded their land and spread disease and still they survived and thrived.

They would make it through the wars and come out stronger. He knew that the reason behind Dark Eagle's urging was to protect his grandson and great-grandson from danger.

The sound of the pots and pans jingling in the wind roused him out of his daydream. "The wind", Blue Moon commented, signaling that she too understood what it meant.

Time to move forward.

Blue Moon watched him from her seated position. It was something about the way he looked holding his son that made her feel safe.

Someone so strong, yet so caring was a rarity from

where she came. She knew that he missed his wife dearly.

He didn't know it, but while he slept late at night, she could hear him talking to his wife. It saddened her. Not because Redd was still in love with his wife, but because he was so very broken and she could tell. She was born to comfort and nurture, yet she had the strength of a bull. She was a Blue Moon.

Her grandmother knew exactly what she was doing when she name her. The story that she once told was of the fire in Blue's eyes the moment she entered the world.

The fire inside of her and the softness of her smile were the most contrasted features her grandmother had ever seen.

She took the baby out of his arms and hugged him close to her chest. As she fed his son, he gathered their things and cleaned up their camp.

Glancing at the old worn map he carried with him on all occasions, Redd sighed. He couldn't understand why his grandfather was taking them straight through the desert.

He didn't have any trouble with the conditions of the desert. They had enough supplies to survive and live well for several months.

It wasn't often that Redd was uneasy about anything. His concern was the inhabitants along the Santa Fe Trail. They would be laying in wait for any unsuspecting travelers. He had to keep his wits about him or they would surely die.

After signaling to Blue Moon that he would return shortly, Redd walked off in search of a his elusive friend. He needed something potent for his arrow tip and only a scorpion would do.

Always prepared for the worst.

Chapter 9

Lemieux vigorously washed the blood off his hands. He had to get moving if he didn't want to get caught and being caught by the law in the tiny Texas town was not his goal. Consequences in Texas lead to being hanged, he was trying his hardest to avoid the gallows.

The night air was crisp and icy. He shivered against it, then fastened his coat around his neck to try and retain some body heat. His body was cold and his heart racing.

He had over $400, which in his mind meant he was rich. That type of money was unheard of to him. Hell, there was a time when he would work in the stables and breaking horses for an entire season and make less than $30.

He successfully found a new way to make an exponential amount of money. This was a new season for Lemieux and he would ensure that it was a profitable one.

$400 in an hour was an enticing sentiment. Stowing the

money away he let out a sigh. He didn't have much further to go before he would have the ransom money and free his family, but all of this fast money really had Lemieux's mind racing.

Sitting at the top of the hill under the cloak of darkness, he stared out at his next target. The stagecoach was due to leave the bank at sunrise the following day. He knew this because the person who bled all over his shoes finally confessed, after he was coaxed with a knife in his side. The bank teller was easy to spot.

Lemieux had been stalking the poor sucker who drove the stagecoach. Observing his movements for several days. He noticed when the bank took in their deposits and when they sent them to the larger bank in Santa Fe, via the stagecoach.

This would be his solution to not only his freedom, but his family's as well.

He couldn't wait to hit it.

Chapter 10

Emil chomped down on his cigar as he glared at the map, hoping that something would jump out at him. If he didn't find out who was stealing from them, he knew that soon it wouldn't just mean his job, but also his life.

"Here ya are", the waitress said placing his whiskey on the table. He took a big gulp and let out a small grunt as the liquid burned his throat going down. He was holding a list of names, Sheriffs and lawmen who he hoped would solve his troubles.

If Trig found out that his businesses were being ravaged like they had. He was hired to take care of this mess, but somehow Emil found himself in a bind. The Sheriff told him that the hit on his stagecoach cost his boss over $2,000.

How was he going to come up with that amount?

He had to replace it. If not, he was sure to be found liable and killed for this mess. Securing business operations was Emil's biggest job role. Instead, he found himself with his hand in the cookie jar. For two years, Emil shaved the proceeds from the Saloon, the bank and the bar that Trig owned. He didn't expect to get caught, why would he?

He was responsible for collecting the funds from each of the three businesses and provide the money to the bank. He had to oversee the transfer of funds from the bank to the stagecoach. Emil was supposed to be standing at the loading area to watch the stagecoach as it was loaded for the trip to Trig's local bank.

Since he was responsible for the receipts and ensuring that the right amount was transported, Emil simply skimmed his extra earnings from the top.

Trig never noticed and he was able to pad his pockets with extra money.

Now things were different.

It wasn't until this recent mess came about that Emil's troubles were exposed. He had to report the exact amount lost to the Sheriff which was a completely different amount than what he told Trig.

The Sheriff also worked for Trig and Emil knew that his accounting mistake would be reported just as the robbery would.

He had to find a way to reach Trig first, with a plan.

He didn't want anyone to know about his transgressions. If Trig found out that he not only dropped the ball on his job, he was stealing money from the company, he would be dead.

Trig was a ruthless man, especially when it came to money.

One mustn't rely solely on tools, the hands and mind are necessities of war…

- Dark Eagle

Chapter 11

Midnight galloped along the dry sandy path as if he knew exactly where they were heading. They rode along the dusty Santa Fe trail for hours without saying one word to each other.

Dark Eagle was speaking to him as they rode, warning him of danger. Redd still hadn't gathered enough courage to ask his grandfather why they were riding through the desert.

Instead, he allowed the soothing voice of Dark Eagle to be his guide. He hummed a northern Sioux melody that his wife used to sing while she prepared their meals.

The large eagle flying overhead squawked as they came to a stop for a moment's rest.

Redd tried his best not to question his grandfather. The Santa Fe trail wasn't an area where one stopped to sight see.

He heard plenty of tails of battles between neighboring tribes and white man, who chose to settle in Texas.

When they came to a stop his companion climbed off the horse and tended to the baby while Redd stretched his legs.

The moon was bright and full.

He studied it, realizing that it was their first Blue Moon in decades. The moon was to light the way through the trail.

His grandfather explained that they would travel under the cloak of darkness. Redd didn't mind.

For some reason he felt more comfortable in darkness. Especially after losing his Catē. He truly missed her. It was times like this where Redd felt alone and deserted.

His Catē would have kept him awake with her tales of her ancestors.

He had to make sure that he was wide awake throughout the journey. The trail had become just as treacherous as it was necessary.

Many tribes along the desert stretch occupied the trail and ensured that passage through the Texan desert was restricted at best.

Redd felt for his secret weapon, his scorpion hiding in a small leather pouch. The scorpion was a deadly, mysterious creature, but it served a great purpose.

The poison located inside the nocturnal insect could kill 100 men and that was his goal.

The feathers on his hat signified his position in the tribe. Redd was a well-accomplished assassin and he did his job quite well.

Unlike the white man who depended on fire power, Redd depended on the lessons taught to him by Dark Eagle.

The tips of his arrows were soaked in venom for nearly three days while the arrows were finely shaven to guarantee deadly precision.

Once Rising Sun was fed Blue began to prepare their meal. She stewed veggies over the hot fire for several minutes, then spooned it into a bowl for Redd to enjoy.

He thanked her and watched as she took a spot next to him. She ate slowly as she watched him enjoy his meal.

There was something peaceful about her and the soothing way she moved. Rocking the baby back and forth, she hummed an ancient song, passed down generations.

Redd recalled the song, his mother used to sing it to him. She and his father were long gone now, along with his grandfather.

He experienced so much loss and hurt in his life, he wondered how long it would take for the winds to change. His thoughts took him to a different place, far away from Texas.

"Blue moon...new beginnings", she said shyly. It took Redd a moment to realize that she was speaking to him. "Yes", he responded never taking his eyes away from the moon. "The new moon means fresh start", she continued.

She continued to rock the baby as she talked, creating a calming effect for not only Rising Sun but Redd Bird. "The ancestors say that any dreams that you dream during the new moon, come true", she recollected staring into his vacant eyes.

Redd's mind was far away from their tiny camp in Santa Fe. At a place of sheer relaxation, his mind wandered to a place and time when he was his happiest. His heart was with Catē.

He realized that she was telling him a story. The more he listened, the more settled he became. It was at this moment where he felt closest to his beloved wife. He could hear her words through Blue Moon's storytelling.

The Eagle that lead the way was perched on the large cactus behind them. Dark Eagle watched over them both day and night. Redd checked their supplies to make sure that he had enough to fully protect them.

That was never a problem, though. Redd could kill with his bare hands, although he didn't rely on his hands often. His grandfather showed him the art of combat, hand-to-hand combat. He used to spar with his cousins and brothers on their lands.

His grandfather's words echoed through the dark night, "One could not rely solely on tools, he must also use his hands and mind to win a war". There was no one wiser than the great Dark Eagle.

Sharpening his spontoon blade pipe tomahawk blade, he

finally allowed himself to relax.

He realized that Blue had finished her story when he noticed the heat from her eyes on his face. "Are you well", she asked quizzically as Redd stared at her in disbelief.

"I'm fine", he responded only then realizing that his face was wet with tears. As they ate in silence, they both relished in the beauty of the Blue Moon.

Smoke from the fire continued to rise to the sky as he lay lazily on the pallet he made from thick blankets. Lemieux wasn't worried about being detected. All he cared about was the money.

This was his victory moment, a time of celebration. He was holding nearly $3,000, more money than he had ever held in his life.

There was a time when Lemieux was a star cowboy, known for roping the biggest longhorn on record in their town. As a youth he was responsible for herding their cows and caring for the livestock with his brothers.

They taught him how to rope and herd like the best of 'em. Lemieux perfected the craft by practicing at night and when the rest of the ranch was resting, Lemieux was putting on a show.

His Pa wanted him to continue in the cowboy profession, but Lemieux wanted more for his life. It was hard out there, especially for a black man. Lemieux faced many challenges both on and off the ranch. He had a superb mount that made other cowboys jealous.

In fact, his skills alone drew the ire of plenty landowners, costing him his job.

Lemieux wanted to be independently wealthy, make his own way without the help of anyone.

Holding the money in his dirty right hand, Lemieux thought of the possibilities. He had a decision to make. His wife was locked away at the home of a savage bandit.

She was taken from their tiny home nearly eight months prior and it was time for Lemieux to put his plan into action.

Now that he knew what he was capable of, he wasn't sure if he wanted to give that all away. Especially, not to get his wife back. The more he considered it, the more ridiculous it all sounded.

Images of Heidi came to his mind as he suddenly shuddered. His wife was a constant nag and a bore to boot.

He gave up a life of breaking wild bucking broncos, but was about to settle into a life of complacency.

He began to wonder if he really wanted it all. The robberies, the investigating and stalking it all brought something different out of Lemieux.

He wasn't the same man that he was that cold winter morning when he realized his Heidi wasn't lying next to him.

He was a different person. As a different person, he wondered if he wanted to return to the same old life.

Lemieux planned the perfect heist, but in order to pull it

off, he would have to enlist some help.

Confident that this could be his big break, he considered his current dilemma.

Whose freedom was more important, his wife or his own?

Life's greatest tragedy is to tiptoe through...hoping to make it safely to death.

- Blue Moon

Chapter 13

"You are wounded", she stated placing her hand over his heart. He nodded agreeing with her. "I know that pain. I feel it every second", she said sadly. "I was once a mother and a wife. I am no longer", she said weeping as Redd stood there staring at her confused.

She then told him the saddest story he'd ever heard. The longer he listened to her speak the more enamored he grew with the troubled young woman. "I awoke to find my husband and my baby gone", she collapsed in tears.

Her husband and child were taken by a rival tribe. It didn't sound like something that would have occurred in their township, but Redd continued to listen to Blue Moon as she told him her tale of woe.

Finally, she wiped her tears and wrapped her arms around Redd in gratitude. Feeling awkward he pushed away.

Looking up at the Blue Moon she sighed loudly, "I am

now beginning new, just like the moon", she replied wiping at her tears. He didn't know what she meant by that, but he did understand her tears.

He comforted the woman, allowing her a place to cry and rest. Although curious, he didn't push her to continue with her story. Redd could tell that whatever pain she held, she wanted to keep hidden.

Emotions had no place in the desert. It was a barren land, one that was meant to be traveled through not immersed in.

He lay awake long after Blue Moon and Rising Sun slept, contemplating his future.

Dark Eagle awoke him before the sun rose. Redd rose with little effort, feeling refreshed for once. He couldn't believe it. It had been months since his sweet Catē died in front of him.

Redd hadn't been able to sleep since that day, until last

night.

He glanced over at his new friend. She looked like sleeping doe, innocent and peaceful. He didn't want to wake her, but he knew that they would have to continue their journey before the heat of the sun made their travel impossible.

Blue Moon slept peacefully with Rising Sun snoring in her arms. He gently roused Blue Moon awake after Midnight was completely packed and ready for the rest of their journey.

It bothered Redd that he didn't have a plan for what he would do once they entered New Mexico. He would have to trust in his grandfather, wholly. It didn't bother him to trust others, it was the blind trust that he had trouble with.

After all, the old man carried them through the desert at one of the most treacherous of times.

Redd knew that the entire trail was wrought with war and battles, he wasn't eager to ride through it, but he knew that everything would be fine.

His grandfather would make sure of it.

Chapter 14

Leaning back in his comfortable chair the lawman listened intently as Emil continued whining about his situation. Smoking on the hand rolled pipe he blew smoke in the squirmy man's face. He didn't respect men who acted like Emil; terrified and in fear, men like that didn't last long in the West.

"How much is in it for me", he asked as the man continued complaining about the money his boss has lost since the beginning. Stanley found it interesting that someone would steal from Trig.

Texas was an enormous place, but not too big that men weren't aware of the food chain when it came to importance. Trig was at the top of the importance food chain.

He wondered who would be so stupid to steal from one of Trig's businesses, but it didn't matter to him. All that mattered to him was Emil's response. "25 dead or alive", he said confidently as Stanley thought it over for a moment.

Reaching his long slender hand out for a firm handshake he smiled at the squirrely man for the firs time since he arrived. "You got yo'self a deal", he said with a grin.

He considered the information given to him by Emil. They had a sketch of the man, given by a bystander at the grocery store. Stanley laughed to himself, hoping that Emil didn't expect him to do much with a drawing.

Stanley had to come up with a plan of his own. If he nabbed the outlaw who was stealing from Trig he could move himself up on the food chain and that was his only goal. Instead of being just a regular old lawman, he would be called Sheriff Stanley and that sounded much better to him than anything.

Once he showed Emil out of the old rickety building, he sat down and began writing out his attack method. He would set a trap so sweet, it would beckon his outlaw from the dark crevices of the dry desert.

He wouldn't know what hit him.

Chapter 15

Emil was ecstatic about Stanley's acceptance for the job. He needed someone to catch this rat before Trig found out the truth and what better person than the cross-eyed lawman under the Sheriff.

Stanley wanted to be Sheriff so bad, Emil could smell it. That was one of the reasons why Emil chose him. An eager deputy beats the real deal any day, they always have something to prove.

He was good at that kind of thing. Reading others was Emil's specialty, that's why he rejoiced greatly when Stanley took the job.

They would have that thieving bastard hung from the nearest gallows in no time.

Emil was sure of it.

Chapter 16

Tipping his hat to the waitress, he walked inside the Saloon and sat in the back at the bar. With two .45 caliber revolvers holstered on both sides, he felt brave enough to tough the current crowd.

The voluptuous woman sashayed towards him with a knowing grin. "Can I get ya something honey", she asked with pleading eyes.

She was a beautiful woman with long brown hair and wide brown eyes, if he wasn't there on business he would have taken her up on her thinly veiled offer.

Instead, he thought about the business at hand. He didn't have time to frolic with the women.

"Whiskey", he grunted as he continued surveying the room. The saloon was pretty crowded for a late evening, making it ripe with gunslingers, outlaws and lawmen alike. This was all perfect for Stanley's plan.

He wanted to be in the middle of the action, listening to the stories and hopefully the clues that others spilled over the bourbon and whiskey.

It was common for businessmen to hire gunslingers and lawmen to protect their assets. Stanley longed for a lucrative job such as that.

He would give his all to make sure someone paid for stealing from Trig.

Chapter 17

After a night of restless sleep, Lemieux had succeeded in making up his mind. He sat across from a man at the bar trading stories about robberies, murders and heists.

While many of the stories were fabrications on Lemieux's part, he suspected differently of his companion.

His new companion introduced himself as Ernest. A local in the town, he was aware of the happenings going on in the small area. He was the type of expert that Lemieux needed to pull the job off.

This gave Lemieux more confidence to share his plan with Ernest.

Since Lemieux was already comfortable using his pistols to kill, he didn't have a problem with him freezing up on him in the middle of the job.

The man stood over seven feet tall and was a broad back

fellow, not as frail looking as Lemieux.

Ernest would be perfect. The new stagecoach driver was a big fella. Lemieux had been watching him for days. The owners replaced the guy that Lemieux killed after his last heist.

He was confident that this fella had no idea how to secure the money and the coach. He and his new friend would bring the perfect element of surprise.

The gruff man had his fair share of gunfights and robberies. Lemieux was impressed. Eager to set his plan into motion he began questioning his companion about holding up the local Saloon after it closed for the night.

"There's gotta be thousands in there", he said nodding towards the large cash register at the front of the building.

The five foot register took up an entire table. Ernest agreed looking around at the already full to capacity

Saloon. It was one of two in the entire town and that meant great business for both.

Both men nodded their heads in agreement with the plan, shaking hands on the idea of working together. Lemieux surmised that there would be at least $1,000 in it for them both.

That made the other man smile broadly; Lemieux being an excellent poker player took that smile as a confirmation of trust.

The men talked and drank for several hours, leaving the bar after dark. He didn't need the liquor, he was high on life at the moment.

Finally, Lemieux was taking the bull by the horns. He was gaining respect in the town.

Lemieux was having the time of his life.

The following night would be his last heist in the Texas town. He wasn't sure if it was the liquor talking but he would gather his Heidi after the heist. Then he would have more than enough money to keep her from kicking his ass.

Chapter 18

The Eagle soared overhead encouraging them to continue riding. Redd could see the opening at the end of the trail with an old wooden sign, welcoming visitors to New Mexico.

Alas they made it, finding out the purpose for the journey was another subject entirely. His guide landed on the cactus in front of them, signaling to Redd Bird and Midnight to stop.

Once they dismounted the horse, they began making camp for the night. Whatever was to come would meet them in the morning, his grandfather warned.

Redd Bird was anxious for the end of the journey, he was exhausted and battle worn.

The following morning he arose to an empty camp and a missing horse. Scratching his head he walked around the spot for several minutes, trying his best to come to grips with it all.

The camp was neatly packed and secured, just as it had been the night before but something was off. Blue and his son were both missing and so were their bags. Redd cried out in sheer agony. The woman took off with his only son.

His face grew dark as his mood changed from confused to angry. Walking off into the New Mexico town he mumbled under his breath.

He was one of the greatest assassins around, he would find her and make her pay for taking his son.

The eagle flying above settled on his shoulder, he would lead the way.

Epilogue

The driver hobbled over to the stable and hitched his horse to the stagecoach. Letting out a sigh he willed himself to hop on the back of the coach.

It had been decades since he drove a stagecoach, he swore that he would never do it again, but somehow he found himself holding the reins once again.

A retired man of 70, Ezra was not looking for work when it found him. His buddy wanted him to drive for him that night, his wife had taken sick and Ezra was the only experienced driver in town.

What could he do, tell him no? He wouldn't have heard the end of it from his wife, so he agreed to take on the job.

The extra $20 that his friend gave him didn't hurt. They were living in a desolate time that money would feed him and his family for three months.

With his aching hip and limited gait, he had to do something to secure more money for them. His oldest son was nearing working age.

He would be 12 soon, old enough to make money for his Ma and Pa. He couldn't wait until that time, then he could finally relax.

"Ahh", he called out to the horses as they galloped along towards his first pickup point. By the time he reached his final destination, he was exhausted. Barely able to lift another heavy bag of coins, he heaved and gave it all he had.

Suddenly, he heard a commotion from behind. Turning to face the commotion, his heart nearly stopped. He was standing in front of two armed men. Ezra nearly messed himself.

He dropped the smaller bag that he was holding and raised his hands as the two men grabbed at the bags, sticking them in one large bag. Ezra watched wide eyed with fear. He knew that the men would kill him, just for being there, he sat silently hoping that they would run off with the money.

As they loaded the last bag the tall man turned to his companion and aimed the gun at his back. "Wh...at...", the man tried to ask as the robber shook his head.

"You should've known better than to fool with the General", Stanley said firing the weapon twice; satisfied that he had finally secured his position at the top of the food chain.

Ezra watched in horror as the man dropped to the ground, dead.

Before he had a chance to say something to the assassin, the man vanished; leaving behind several gold coins and a wanted poster with the dead man's picture on the front.